A DEADLY MISTAKE

The window shattered with a splintering crash of glass. Elizabeth screamed, in fright or perhaps in an effort to distract Blade. She tried to drag Blade down, but he could take no chances. His knee came up sharply into her stomach and he jerked himself free. As she fell to the floor, two gunmen carrying Soviet-made dart-throwers came charging into the room.

Blade sidestepped the men so fast they had no chance to draw a bead on him. One man screamed, as Blade spun him around and twisted his arm out of the socket. Before the other gunman could fire a shot, the edge of Blade's right hand came down like an executioner's axe. The gun landed next to Elizabeth, but the man made the mistake of looking at her for a fraction of a second too long.

Blade's fingers closed on the dartgun as new sounds exploded outside. There was the unmistakable *whooom* of a gasoline tank igniting, and a second later a long, terrible scream. Then came silence.

"I think my friends have just taken care of the rest of your friends, Elizabeth."

"What—what about me?"

The Blade Series:

HEROIC FANTASY SERIES **17**

BLADE
THE MOUNTAINS OF BREGA
by Jeffrey Lord

PINNACLE BOOKS • NEW YORK CITY

This is a work of fiction. All the characters and events portrayed in this book are fictional, and any resemblance to real people or incidents is purely coincidental.

BLADE: THE MOUNTAINS OF BREGA

Copyright © 1976 by Lyle Kenyon Engel

An original Pinnacle Books edition, published for the first time anywhere.

ISBN: 0-523-00812-0

First printing, February 1976

Cover illustration by Tran Mawicke

Printed in the United States of America

PINNACLE BOOKS, INC.
275 Madison Avenue—
New York, N.Y. 10016

THE MOUNTAINS OF BREGA

1

Richard Blade was bored. This condition very seldom killed anybody. It did not very often make people want to die. But it could and did take away much of a man's zest for living. At the moment, it was doing that to Richard Blade.

He turned on the heel of one custom-made shoe and stared out the floor-to-ceiling window of the deluxe flat. The peach-colored velvet draperies were drawn back, and through the heavy glass he could see London spread out below. The flat was forty stories up in one of the newest of London's luxury buildings, so Blade could see a long way. The twinkling lights and spots of color that were neon signs seemed to march endlessly away into the darkness. It was an unusually clear night, but the spectacle did nothing to diminish Blade's boredom.

From behind him came the noises of a cocktail party. Ice cubes clinked in glasses, corks popped, soda-water siphons hissed like snakes. The noises simply made Blade feel more bored. They were so expected, so conventional.

Blade was at the party more out of a sense of duty than anything else. He was there as the guest of a certain young lady who wanted to show him off to her "set." She had been quite frank about that. She hadn't been quite as frank about why she was showing him off. But Blade had an almost instinctive ability to read another person's intentions toward him. He wouldn't have been alive without it. And what he read in Clarissa was the desire to snare him for a husband.

He was certainly eligible enough. The Richard Blade who moved elegantly through the London social whirl was one of the most eligible bachelors around. Wit, charm, intelligence, and an ample if vague income—he had them all. Though he had left forty behind, his face and body showed no signs that he was much more than thirty. Not a confirmed bachelor, in other words—still young enough for a determined woman to mold into whatever kind of husband might strike her fancy.

The faint reflection from the window glass gave Blade a picture of his face and body. It was a strong face—the face of a warrior rather than a courtier. Blade had been both in his career, in places stranger and more distant than anyone in the room could or would believe even if he chose to tell them.

And the body inside the custom-tailored jacket—that was an athlete's body, six feet one and a little more, carrying two hundred and ten pounds on its large bones. It suggested a former rowing or tennis Blue from Oxford who had kept himself in excellent trim. Blade had been those, among other things.

Now he was almost physically itching with boredom. He looked at his reflection in the window again and noticed a pale face framed in dark hair hovering near his right shoulder. He drained the last of his drink and turned to face the slender woman who had drifted up behind him as he stared out the window.

She must have been at least five feet eight. Her dark brown hair swept up to a point almost on a level with the top of Blade's head, and her wide gray eyes looked almost straight into his. From her grooming and poise, Blade thought at first that she might be a fashion model. But her figure was too full in the hips and bosom, and her legs were too elegantly curved to make her a good object on which to hang current fashions.

She smiled as she sensed his eyes going over her. "You look bored, I think. Yes?" There was a slight trace of a foreign accent in her low voice. Blade

2

tried to place it. Not French; not Italian. German? Vaguely, but not quite. Somewhere farther to the east? Quite possibly. Without any outwardly visible sign, Blade was on the alert.

"Rather," he drawled. He wanted to sound a little like the stereotyped silly-ass English playboy. A little, but not too much.

The woman smiled again. "My name is Elizabeth." The *b* sounded almost like a *v*. "You are—?"

"Blade. Richard Blade. I'm a friend of Clarissa's."

"Ah, another one of the men she brings around to show off."

"You know her?"

"For several years I have known her. She helped me a lot when I first came to England."

"Where did you come from?" The question slipped out before it occurred to him that it might be untactful. If the woman had come to England from somewhere behind the Iron Curtain, she might not wish to talk about her reasons for doing so.

"I am Czech," said Elizabeth. "I was in England in 1968 when the Russians marched into my country, and I did not want to go back. Clarissa helped me very much, to find a job and get settled. I owe her a good deal. But I cannot think much of the way she is always showing off her men friends."

"Like a hunter, showing off trophies?"

Elizabeth laughed. "Yes, exactly." She looked Blade over from head to foot, the same way he had done her. Then she smiled and said, "This time I think she has caught a good one."

Blade couldn't help smiling, even though the flattery was rather transparent. Listening to an attractive woman say things like that to him was always pleasant, even if he suspected she was playing games. And he did suspect Elizabeth. He decided to draw her out a little more.

"Actually, I wouldn't say I've been caught, not really," he said.

3

"You and Clarissa are—just good friends, I think the saying goes?"

Blade nodded. He made a mental note that Elizabeth was not a very skilled player, unless her game was something he couldn't even imagine. She was too eager, too fast with her answers. He was not going to have much chance to reveal himself—unless they wound up in bed. That was all right with him. But he was going to keep on the alert, no matter how the evening ended.

Elizabeth threw her head back and smiled warmly at Blade. The motion thrust her full breasts out even farther against the red wool of her dress. Blade didn't need to keep his eyes off those breasts and didn't try. The woman noticed where his eyes were.

To give the impression of being entirely at ease, Blade said, "Would you like another drink?" He pointed at the woman's empty glass.

"I would, but not any more of Clarissa's. I still can't get used to Scotch or mixed drinks. I have a better idea. I have some real Czech brandy in my apartment. Why don't we go over there and try that?"

"Why not, indeed?" said Blade, with a grin. He did his best to make it a mindlessly lecherous grin, but his mind was turning with almost audible clicks. Elizabeth's game of getting him to her apartment was transparently obvious. Why was she playing it, and playing it so crudely? Was it just plain and simple lust for a handsome man, or something more? Richard Blade had been a professional secret agent for far too long to rule out the possibility of something more.

But he would never find out either way if he didn't accept Elizabeth's invitation. He took her hand and squeezed it with a firm but gentle pressure. "I'll make my apologies to Clarissa, and then we can go. Is your apartment far?"

Elizabeth nodded and named an address about four miles away.

"Then we'll take my car. Do you mind riding in an MG?"

4

"Not at all." She looked at him again, with obvious invitation in her eyes. "Somehow a sports car—it fits you, what I think you are."

Blade made his way over to the bar and went through the routine of saying goodbye to Clarissa. He was glad that Elizabeth had agreed to ride with him. One telephone call to the man known as J, one twist of a concealed switch, and the Special Branch of the Metropolitan Police would be tracking him all the way to his destination.

Elizabeth clung tightly to his arm as they rode down in the elevator, flashing increasingly warm smiles at him all the while. In the lobby of the building he excused himself. "I need to make a phone call—tell the office I may be late tomorrow." He looked at her as he said that, watching for any reaction.

All he could see was a small frown, making a faint crease in the high, pale forehead. "I thought you had an independent income, Mr. Blade."

Blade did not snap "Where did you learn that?" but it was a close call. He could not avoid stiffening slightly, however. He had not mentioned one word about his living in their conversation. Elizabeth's question was a definite clue—a nasty one, too.

But he was calm again within seconds. He merely said, "Oh, I do. But the chaps at Consolidated Jute seem to think my father's son is worth something. So I go into the Production Division's office two or three days a week. Mostly, I've better ways to spend my time. But I do have to make that call." He gently pulled himself free from her arm and strode across the lobby toward the public phone behind one of the marble columns.

It was virtually impossible that this public phone could be tapped by the opposition, so Blade was not worried about his brief message getting to the wrong ears as he spoke into the phone.

"J—Traveler here. Bodkin falling. Listen."

In plain English:

"J—this is Richard Blade. I think somebody's trying

5

to entrap me. I'm turning on the homer in my car. Alert the Special Branch men and have them trace it and follow me." He had no need to worry either about the message not being passed on. Any of his cryptic call-signs would trigger the alarm on J's telephone monitor and have the old spymaster on the move in minutes. The head of the secret intelligence division MI6 had not lived as long or risen as high as he had by letting critical messages slip by him.

Secure in the knowledge that he had alerted the appropriate people, Blade rejoined Elizabeth. His hand found her arm again. This time her hand squeezed back with more warmth than before. Hand in hand, they walked out to the garage where Blade had parked his MG. They climbed in, and Blade started up the engine, then turned to Elizabeth.

"Would you like a cigarette?"

"No, thank you."

"Mind if I smoke, then?"

"Not at all."

Blade reached into the breast pocket of his coat for a gold-plated cigarette case and extracted a Benson & Hedges. With his other hand he reached for the cigarette lighter and shoved it in. As he did so, he also gave it a small twist to the left. With that twist, a solid-state circuit was completed, and the car's electronic tracer went on. Then he lit the cigarette, shoved the lighter back into its socket, and put the car in motion.

By the MG's odometer, the four miles Elizabeth had mentioned were more like six. They were well out into the southwest corner of London before they stopped. For the last half of the trip they had followed a zigzag course, turning at irregular intervals down dark side streets. It was a course that made no sense at all, unless Elizabeth was trying to shake off any car that might be trailing them. Several times Blade caught her looking intently into the side-view mirror. If Elizabeth was an agent for the opposition, she was a remarkably clumsy one. Or she was a highly skilled agent pretending to be clumsy to catch him off guard. That had happened before. In fact, Blade himself had done it more than once.

Eventually Elizabeth gestured to the middle one of a trio of Victorian townhouses. Once they had been the modestly luxurious residences of city merchants or bankers; now they had fallen, if not exactly on evil days, at least on less prosperous ones. Blade could see peeling paint, unwashed windows, and untended front lawns under the dim streetlamps.

In fact, the lamplight was so dim that Blade was fully alert as they climbed out of the car. The half-dark street and the totally dark alleys could easily hide enough men to ambush a platoon. But they reached the door, climbed the stairs, and entered Elizabeth's third-floor flat without incident. The name on the flat's door was *Elizabeth Hruska*. A good enough Czech name.

The flat was an ordinary bed-sitter, with the luxury of a modern kitchen—or at least a modern stove—and a halfway modern bath. Elizabeth waved one hand toward the couch by the kitchen door. "Make yourself at home, Mr.—Richard. The brandy is in the cabinet over the refrigerator. I am going to get out of this dress before I roast in it."

As Elizabeth had suggested, Blade went to the cupboard. The brandy was there, a Czech brand Blade recognized as highly reputable. He poured out two glasses and cautiously sniffed at both of them. Then he quickly scanned the kitchen. There were more places than he could count where a concealed microphone or even a concealed lens might be lurking. He could never search them all, even if he wanted to.

And Blade didn't want to. He didn't want to give any observers the idea that he was a trained professional at this game—which he had been for nearly twenty years. He wanted to let them think he was a fat and unsuspecting fly that had blundered into their web. At least until the time came for them to discover that they had blundered into *his*. He grinned.

7

The spider-versus-spider games of espionage had been his life so long that he could hardly help enjoying it.

The kitchen window opened onto a rust-scarred iron fire escape. Blade looked up and down it as far as he could without opening the window. He noticed that the window locked from the inside. That was usual in this neighborhood. But the lock was open—not usual in this neighborhood. With his eyes on the kitchen door, he carefully flipped the lock closed. Anybody coming down the fire escape and expecting an easy entrance through the kitchen window would get a surprise.

Blade picked up the two glasses of brandy, went back into the sitting room, and sat down on the couch. As an afterthought, he took off his coat and tie and unbuttoned the collar of his hand-made silk shirt. He didn't need anything in the coat, since he did not go armed in England. He hardly needed to, in any case—not with a fourth *dan* black belt in karate.

The sound of bare feet on the carpet made him look up. Elizabeth had indeed taken off her dress, and practically everything else she had been wearing. Now she wore a long, flowing nightdress, with full-length sleeves and a high neck. It did not conceal very much, however, for it was semi-transparent. Blade did not need to imagine what Elizabeth's body was like any longer. It was a full-fleshed East European body, a hearty young peasant girl's body. Large breasts thrust out the fabric of the nightdress, and proportionately large nipples thrust out even farther as the breasts swayed.

Blade rose to his feet and held out his arms as she approached, with a broad grin on his face. He would have worn that grin even if he had not found her attractive. But Blade was a man of large appetites and a large capacity for pleasure. He had never been able to make love in a cool or detached manner.

Elizabeth took his hands, and a smile spread across her face, telling Blade that she knew exactly what was on his mind. He hoped she didn't know what he was really thinking—when would her confederates make their move, if they were going to make one? And what kind of move would it be? Was this just a blackmail effort, or were enemy agents really going to try a body-snatch on him?

Elizabeth was picking up her brandy glass, and Blade decided not to try answering those questions. He took his own glass, raised it to clink with hers, and said, "Cheers."

She smiled. "To a good night's work," she said, and giggled. Then she drained the glass at one gulp. Blade considered the nervous note in her giggle and the gulped brandy. She wasn't quite able to keep up the air of cheerful sensuality that she was trying to project—at least not without a quick drink. It was long odds that this girl was an amateur, caught in something far beyond her depth. How and why? Another question he wasn't going to answer now.

Blade emptied his own glass in five deliberate swallows and set it down on the arm of the couch. It was good brandy; he had to admit that. Then his arms rose again, and reached out for Elizabeth.

She was in them before he had them fully raised. A moment later her lips were clinging to his. Those lips were wide open, but there was no warmth or wetness on them or in them. For a moment the sudden shock of those lips against his almost killed Blade's desire. Then Elizabeth's hands came up and locked around the back of his neck. They drew his head forward and down, played in his chair, crept down under his collar. One hand moved away from his neck and around to his throat. Slim but nimble fingers undid the buttons of his shirt from the top down. Then they roamed over the muscle-layered chest and flat stomach, for Blade wore no undershirt.

If Elizabeth was doing this against her inclinations, she was not letting that stand in the way of doing it well. Blade felt his breath beginning to come fast, and felt a familiar warm ache swelling in his groin. He knew that if he looked down there would be another and more visible swelling in the front of his dark blue pants.

Elizabeth did look down. The hand that had been stroking Blade's chest moved down to where her eyes were aimed. The fingers stroked momentarily in this new place, then closed on Blade's zipper. A sharp metallic *zzzzt*, and the same fingers were reaching in to close around Blade's swollen member.

They were just as skilled there as they had been higher up. In fact, they were almost unbearable when they got inside Blade's shorts and began playing with his bare flesh. He had to bite back a gasp. Then he managed to grate out:

"For God's sake—you're half-naked—let me—" He was partly pretending to be half out of his mind with desire, but only partly.

Elizabeth understood and stepped away from him while he struggled out of his clothes. The sound of ripping cloth told him of another shirt gone to hell, but he was long past caring. Kicking and hurling his clothes wildly in all directions, in a few seconds he was wearing even less than Elizabeth.

Her eyes widened in unmistakable admiration at the sight of Blade's physique. It was an admiration as genuine as Blade's own arousal, but Blade knew that nothing would keep Elizabeth from carrying out whatever job she had been given—if any.

If any. Blade found himself hoping that the whole idea of an attempt against him was simply the result of his own overworked imagination. Elizabeth promised a first-class tumble, and damn it, he didn't want things complicated by anyone barging into the middle of it. He bloody well didn't!

He started to take Elizabeth in his arms again, but she pushed him away. Then she jerked the nightdress over her head. Before she could raise her hands again, Blade's arms closed around her, running down the satiny skin of her back to cup her full, round buttocks and pull her hard against him. She swallowed and threw her head back as his lips dipped to caress her hroat. Her long hair fell down over her shoulders, whispering softly as their movements tossed it about. Blade felt his erection surge still higher, pressing firmly against her.

Then the kitchen window shattered with a splintering crash of glass. The sound of a human voice cursing in pain followed, then the thud of a body falling onto the kitchen floor.

Elizabeth screamed, in fright or perhaps in an effort to distract Blade. She tried to cling to Blade, dragging his arms down. He could take no chances now. His knee came up sharply into her stomach. At the same time he jerked both arms free and shoved hard. Elizabeth staggered back, half doubled over, then sat down on the rug with a thump, holding her stomach. As she did so, two men came charging out of the kitchen at a run.

Both wore workmen's clothes, but carried guns. Blade recognized the guns as Soviet-made dart throwers. And both the gunmen moved with the assured competence of men as fully professional as Blade himself.

Blade sidestepped the men so fast they had no chance to draw a bead on him. He darted across the path of the left-hand man, then closed. The man dropped into fighting stance and tried to bring his gun around. But he could not turn fast enough to match Blade's lightning reflexes. Blade's hands darted out and clamped shut. The man spun around again, but this time he let out a scream as Blade twisted his arm out of its socket. Then Blade's foot came up, smashing into the small of the man's back and sending him flying across the room.

He did not hit his comrade, but he did make the other flinch back and lose the aim he was drawing on Blade. Before the dart gun could swing to cover him and fire, Blade had closed with the second man. The edge of his right hand came down like an executioner's axe, and the gun went flying. It landed within easy reach of Elizabeth, but the man made the mistake of

11

looking at Elizabeth for a fraction of a second too long. In that moment Blade leaped high in a karate spring-kick, driving his left foot into the man's stomach. Like a cannonball the man flew backward to crash into the wall. And like a half-empty sack he sagged limply down onto the floor.

Blade pivoted as he came down, then lunged at the dart gun. His fingers closed on it as new sounds exploded outside. Five gunshots erupted in rapid succession, two shotgun blasts, a brief sputter of automatic weapons. There was the unmistakable *whoooom* of a gasoline tank igniting, and a second later a long and terrible scream. The scream ended in a squashy *thump*, and after that came silence.

Blade picked Elizabeth up, carried her unresisting body to the couch, and pulled the nightdress back over her head. By the time he had retrieved a decent minimum of his own clothing, her eyes were beginning to focus again and her breathing had almost returned to normal. His voice was clipped and cool as he spoke to her.

"I think my friends have just taken care of the rest of your friends."

"My friends?" she said dully.

"Yes. I don't know who they are, but we'll find out shortly. Those two with the dart guns, at least, are going to live to be questioned."

"What—what about me?" she said, with a faint whimper.

"That depends. If you cooperate—"

"But my family—oh, God, why didn't I just kill myself when they asked me? Why, why, why?" And she burst into tears.

Blade could not help feeling sorry for her. Unless she was still acting, she had just confirmed his suspicions that she was an amateur, dragged into posing as bait by blackmail or threats. Now he had to find out who had done the blackmailing or threatening. And it was even more important to find out how much they knew about Richard Blade, and why they were after him.

If they were after him because he had been one of the best and deadliest agents of MI6 for twenty years, that was one thing. There were several like him. But if they were after him because they knew or suspected his role in Project Dimension X—that was something far different, far worse.

It was far worse because Richard Blade was the only living man who could travel into other dimensions.

2

There were four people in the office. They were the only four people in the world who were supposed to know all about Project Dimension X. There was Richard Blade, the project's front-line soldier. He had made sixteen trips into Dimension X. No other living man had made even one and returned alive and sane. There were hopes that someone might turn up sooner or later, but so far all the searching had not disclosed that someone.

There was Lord Leighton, as brilliant as he was temperamental, Britain's leading computer scientist. The great computers under the Tower of London that sent Blade into Dimension X were his creation. His small dark eyes behind their thick glasses flicked irritably around the room. Occasionally he would shift position in his chair, trying to get more comfortable. That was hard, with a body distorted by polio, a hunchback, and eighty-odd years.

J returned Leighton's glance imperturbably. Everything about J seemed ordered and disciplined, even the lines in his face and the iron-gray hair receding from his high forehead. The imperturbability was not a pose, either. J had been a spy and then a spymaster for all the years of a career that went back to World War I. If he had been the type to lose his head, he would long since have been dead. He had picked Richard Blade out of Oxford, watched his career as an MI6 agent for nearly twenty years, then seen him move on to Project Dimension X. He was never happy about seeing the man he loved like a son hurled off

14

into the unknown. But neither he nor Blade would ever balk at doing for England what needed to be done.

Nor would the fourth man in the room, the Prime Minister. He seldom sat in on these policy conferences for the project. He did not understand most of what was discussed, and admitted as much. He was a skilled politician, not a spymaster, scientist, or man of action. He held the pursestrings, tried to satisfy the project's voracious appetite for money, and kept an eye on the big picture. That last was why he was here now. A threat to the security of the project was a threat to the security of England, and perhaps to the whole free world.

"—so the men themselves have no apparent ties with any foreign government," J was saying.

Before J could go on, the Prime Minister interrupted him. "Does that mean we needn't worry about major security leaks?"

J shook his head more sharply than usual. Silly questions of that sort had annoyed the older man as long as Blade had known him. "It means nothing of the kind. I said 'no *apparent* ties.' We have to dig deeper. And there's the girl, Elizabeth."

Blade stiffened slightly in his seat. It was damned unprofessional of him, to be sure, but he was concerned about that poor girl.

J gave him a reassuring smile. "She says she was pushed into it by a threat to her family. They're still in Czechoslovakia. So if the people who threatened her aren't Soviet agents themselves, they're certainly working for somebody who's in contact with the Soviet intelligence apparatus."

"What about one of the big industrial espionage firms?" put in Blade. "I wouldn't put it past some of them to try a caper like this, if the money was right."

"Neither would I," said J sourly. "We're checking that possibility right now."

"But what about Elizabeth herself?" asked Blade.

Again J smiled. "We've tested her story every way we could. She seems to be telling the truth. We're going to push an inquiry back through our Czech network to get further confirmation. If that also puts her in the clear, we're going to stop worrying about her. We'll give her a new identity and arrange for her to emigrate to Canada without any fuss or bother. Of course we'll be keeping her under surveillance for a year or two, but that will be more for her own protection than ours."

Blade could not hold back a sigh of relief, which drew another smile from J. Then the older man's manner became brisk and businesslike again.

"We'll push inquiries about the gunmen themselves in every possible direction," he went on. "I'd rather not compromise any of our key people, of course, but if necessary . . ." He left the sentence unfinished, but Blade at least could fill in the missing words with no difficulty. "In any case, it will be a considerable aid to us if MOD can also move on the matter." He looked at the PM.

The PM nodded. "Certainly. Ministry of Defense has as much of a stake in this as anybody else. But it's going to mean delaying MOD support for some of the related projects, like the new people and the training center."

"Right now, they're not that important," said J. Blade knew that statement must be costing the other man a good deal. For years J had dreamed above all of finding someone else besides Blade to travel into Dimension X. "If the project has been seriously compromised, we're going to have some very hard decisions to make."

"Not to mention expensive," said the Prime Minister sourly. He knew from long and weary experience that any major changes in the operation of a project this size usually carried a price tag in six figures.

"I'm afraid so," said J bluntly. "Then there's Richard. I doubt if there's going to be another attempt to snatch him soon, not with our investigation hopefully putting the opposition on the defensive. But I'd feel a great deal better if he were somewhere they couldn't

16

possibly get at him for a while. And I can't think of any better place than Dimension X." He looked at Lord Leighton. "How soon could you set up the computer to send Richard off?"

Lord Leighton considered the matter for a few seconds. Then he shrugged his thin, bowed shoulders. "I was planning to down-line the main computer for about ten days to incorporate some of the Controlled Return devices. But if all you want is the conventional techniques—well, what about tomorrow?"

"Tomorrow will be fine," said Blade.

"Then tomorrow it is," said J.

And it was the next morning when Blade presented himself at the Tower of London. The Special Branch men, clothing as dark as the gray sky overhead, led him to the head of the secret elevator. The massive bronze doors closed behind him, and the elevator car plunged two hundred feet straight down to the level of the secret complex below the tower.

This morning J was too busy with his investigations to see Blade off. So Blade walked down the long, gleaming corridor and through the electronically guarded doors by himself. He heard the clatter of typewriters and the faint murmur of laboratory equipment from behind closed doors on either side as he walked. But he met no one until he reached the door to the central complex. There Lord Leighton himself met Blade.

"Ah, Richard," the scientist said with a grin. "Prompt as usual. I started the main sequence ten minutes ago, assuming you'd be on time. And I was right. You'd have made a first-class scientist, Richard. You've got the proper taste for precision."

Blade smiled. "Perhaps. But I don't think I have some of the other gifts." Lord Leighton was unbending more than usual, but Blade didn't really feel much like conversation. He was always more or less on edge as he approached the moment of being hurled into Dimension X. And the attempt on his life still bothered

17

him somewhat. He lived with danger in Dimension X, but it was a long time since he had been in any danger here in England.

As always, the ritual of preparing for the journey eased the strain. Blade went into the small changing room and stripped to his skin. Then he smeared every square inch of that skin with a foul-smelling black grease, used to prevent electrical burns from the massive jolt of current that would be passing through his body. Then he knotted a loincloth about his waist. That never did anything to justify the trouble of putting it on—Blade had always arrived in Dimension X naked as a newborn baby.

Greased and clothed, Blade stepped out of the room and walked across the main computer chamber. The huge consoles of the computer loomed above him. Their gray, crackled finish absorbed most of the light in the chamber. At times Blade felt that there was an alien and sinister intelligence lurking invisibly in those consoles, an intelligence that dwarfed not only his own but Lord Leighton's as well. This chamber could make a man believe in tales of Frankenstein's monsters and mad scientists.

Lord Leighton would certainly do well enough for the mad scientist. Dressed in his usual rumpled and filthy laboratory smock, he scuttled about among the consoles, long-fingered hands darting over switches and buttons, eyes taking in dial readings.

Eventually he was satisfied that his precious and temperamental computers could be left alone for a few moments. Then he came over to Blade's chair and began attaching cobra-headed metal electrodes to every imaginable part of Blade's body. By the time Leighton had finished, Blade looked as though he were being attacked by a rainbow-colored horde of tiny snakes. The wires ran off in clusters into the computer consoles. Blade sat back as far as the electrodes would let him and relaxed as much as he could.

He did not have to wait long. The computer flowed

18

steadily and without a single hitch this time. Minutes later, Leighton turned to Blade with a smile on his face.

"Ready, Richard?"

Blade gave a thumbs-up signal with both hands. Leighton's right hand rose, hovered over the red master switch for a moment, then descended. The switch came down also, sliding to the bottom of its metal slot.

As the switch reached bottom, the whole chamber seemed to turn upside down. The stone floor was overhead, with the chair and computer consoles hanging from it. Beside one of the consoles, Blade saw Lord Leighton standing motionless, head down, looking like some misshapen, white-furred bat. Far below Blade's head lay the raw, gray rock of the ceiling.

It seemed to be getting farther and farther away, too. Gradually the grayness below faded away. Now there was only blackness, with vague, swirling red shapes. Blade could no longer feel the chair against him or the electrodes on his body, but his eyes told him that he was still hanging head down from that chair.

The red shapes below became brighter and began to drive away the blackness. They seemed to be alive, darting and leaping about purposefully. Then they became still brighter and more distinct. As they took shape, Blade felt a cold chill run through him. They were monstrous fanged heads, swaying on the ends of long, serpent-like necks, opening gaping black maws. And he was hanging helpless, exposed to them like a ripe fruit on a branch. How long would it be before the darting monsters below noticed him, lunged upward, plucked him down?

One of them lifted its head, the mouth wide open, with silvery teeth shimmering in a ring around the gaping black center. The head grew larger; the mouth grew wider. Blade found it hard to keep his own mouth from opening in a scream of terror.

19

The head rose up to him. A shock ran through Blade's body. Everywhere he looked, the silver teeth were gleaming, as the mouth closed on him. Then there was no more color, no red, no silver—only blackness.

3

Blade could not even guess how long the total blackness around him lasted. In the blackness he was without sight, without hearing, without sensation of any kind.

Then suddenly all his senses returned. He also had the same splitting headache he always had when he arrived in Dimension X. He tried to roll over—and froze abruptly as he felt the springy surface beneath him lurch and sway sickeningly. The motion did not help the condition of his head or his stomach. His hands searched on either side of him for something to grip, and closed around needle-heavy branches. He held on grimly until the swaying ended and his headache began to fade. Then he realized that the scent of needles and resin was heavy, almost overpowering, in his nostrils. And more needles were pricking into his bare back. Slowly, a bit at a time, he rolled over on his stomach.

As Blade saw what lay below, he let out a sigh of relief. He had landed on the branch of a tree. But the ground was only ten feet below, and it was thickly covered with moss and fallen needles. He could have plunged straight down into it and landed safely, as if he had fallen into a feather bed. Satisfied that he wasn't going to fall out of the tree like a mislaid bird's egg and smash himself to pieces, he lay back on the branch until his headache had completely gone. Then he rolled over on his back and looked up.

The tree seemed to soar skyward forever, its top lost in a green maze of jutting branches. The branches were heavy with needles, and at each fork hung a

21

large cluster of cones. Far above—how far Blade couldn't even guess—he could see patches of blue sky. Sunlight shot through those gaps, faintly gilding some of the needles.

Blade decided there was no point in sitting perched on the branch like an abandoned bird's nest. He wasn't going to meet any of the inhabitants of this dimension up here. Unless they were birds or monkeys, perhaps? He grinned at the thought. Then slowly he began to back down the branch toward the trunk of the tree. No matter how soft the landing might be, he would rather climb down than jump.

He reached the trunk and got ready to swing himself down from the branch. Then suddenly he froze, listening intently. His trained hearing had picked up the sound of approaching footsteps, off to the right. They were approaching slowly and stealthily, which suggested to Blade that the visitors were stalking something. He didn't want it to become him.

Blade decided that the tree had suddenly become a very good place to stay. With a quick jerk of his powerful arms, he pulled himself back up on the branch. In moments he was hidden from the sight of anyone on the ground unless they were looking very carefully. Holding on with both hands, he peered down through the gaps in the needles, listening to the footsteps. It sounded like a fair-sized party—five or more—and they definitely were trying to tread lightly.

A moment later Blade saw a flicker of movement approaching through the greenery. He held his breath as eight young women passed below in single file. They moved with long, graceful, slow steps, placing their feet carefully to avoid stepping on twigs. All wore tunics and trousers of heavy cloth, spotted green and brown like camouflage suits of a Home Dimension army, and moccasin-like sandals. One had her tunic tied by the sleeves around her neck, and was bare to the waist.

All eight carried a short sword and dagger in their belts, and seven carried bows and quivers slung over their backs. The eighth—the apparent leader—carried a spear with a tuft of gold feathers tied around it. All eight also carried bulging brown leather sacks slung over their backs.

If Blade had doubted that this was a hunting party, he had no doubts now. But he still wasn't sure what they were hunting, and he still didn't want it to be him. It was also a little unusual for a hunting party to be made up entirely of women.

Unless this was a dimension or at least a people where women ruled. That was a distinct possibility, and not a particularly welcome one. Female-dominated societies were not necessarily more dangerous or hostile than male-dominated ones, but they were hardly ever less so, either. As far as war and cutthroat politics were concerned, Blade knew women were completely equal!

The eight women passed below Blade and out into the clearing visible on his left. Now he had to raise his head slightly and shift position in order to see them clearly. He did both reluctantly, not at all inclined to accidentally surprise the women and wind up punctured by their arrows before he could explain himself.

The women were slinging the brown leather sacks off their backs now, opening them, and shaking out the contents onto the ground. There were weighted cords, things that looked like rolled-up nets, small axes that winked in the sunlight, and several large jars. The leader began pulling the stoppers out of the jars, and a powerful odor of something rich and sweet filled the clearing. Even up on his branch, Blade found it almost unpleasantly strong.

It did not appear to bother the women at all. Now they took off their moccasins and began moving barefooted about the clearing. It was obvious that they were trying not to disturb even the smallest leaf. Carefully they picked up the jars and set them in a wide circle that covered most of the clearing. Then, one by one, they slipped behind the trees around

23

the clearing. Blade's trained eyes saw faint flickers of movement in the shade and the greenery as they settled down to wait. The trap was laid and baited. Now there was nothing for either Blade or the women to do but wait for the quarry to appear. Blade shifted position slightly, away from a branch that was digging into his ribs.

Time passed. The light from above no longer gilded the needles so brightly or came down at quite the same angle. The day was moving on. Sweat ran down Blade's body and attracted small insects. All whined maddeningly, and some of them bit or stung. High above, the *chrrrreeek* of a large bird or tree-dwelling animal sounded through the forest.

Then the breeze became stronger, making the needles whisper more loudly and the branch sway more. It dried the sweat from Blade's skin and drove the insects away, but it also forced him to hold on harder. And it suggested that the coming night might be chilly—too chilly for the comfort or safety of a naked man. But even so, Blade still did not care to risk unnecessarily the arrows of the huntresses below. He shifted again to ease cramped limbs, listening to the branch creak under him and smelling the odor of whatever was in the bait pots.

Then once again he caught a flicker of movement off to the right. There was something about the movement suggesting raw, careless, animal strength, rather than the stalking pace of the women. Whoever or whatever was approaching was certainly making no effort to keep quiet. Blade heard a steadily swelling chorus of grunts, growls, and half-verbalized mutterings. He began to hear heavy footsteps and a continuous cracking of twigs and rustle of leaves.

Then Blade saw the approaching party through a gap in the curtain of needles. There were four of them, and Blade's first startled question to himself was—man or ape? Certainly they had shaggy pelts more like a gorilla's than anything else, large, knob-knuckled hands on unnaturally long arms, and low foreheads with massive ridges of bone over the eyes. But they walked erect, occasionally turning their heads from side to side to sniff the air. They communicated by means of real speech, not just animal growls. And each carried a stout club slung by a leather thong from a leather belt around his waist. These men were Neanderthal level or perhaps even more primitive, definitely far below whatever level the women represented. But they were certainly men.

It also began to look as if they were the intended prey of the huntresses. Blade tensed in anticipation of a sudden explosion of violence in the peaceful clearing below. His eyes drifted from the wild men to the trees that concealed the women lying in ambush. They had covered their tracks well, but perhaps the men would scent them—or him. That was an unpleasant thought. The wild men looked even less likely to give him a peaceful reception than the women did.

Blade suddenly realized what the purpose of the sweetness in the pots was. Not only was it bait; its strong odor would overwhelm any lingering traces of the scent of the women, and make the wild men careless.

It was doing just that right now. The four men were scurrying across the clearing with cries of delight, like children let out of school. Each of them headed straight to one of the pots and squatted down beside it. With more cheerful cries and hoots, they thrust their massive hands inside and began scooping out the contents. It was a thick, sticky paste, semi-translucent like crystallized honey, with white crystals of sugar in it.

The wild men ate greedily, cramming the paste into their mouths in enormous dripping handfuls, then gulping it down with frantic workings of mouth and throat. Blade had the impression that the paste was a rare treat for them. So rare, in fact, that the desire to cram down as much of it as they could wiped out all thoughts of possible danger. Blade shook his head in half-amused frustration. He was tempted to warn the wild men, but would the warning penetrate their hunger-fogged minds even if he gave it? And what would the women do then, the women lying in wait behind the trees?

Moments later, the women were no longer lying in wait. Like eight graceful cats, they leaped out from their hiding places. Each had her short sword drawn, but carried it in her left hand. In her right hand each swung one of the weighted cords.

Still absorbed in their feast, the wild men were fatally slow to react. Before more than one of them could raise his hand or turn around, the weighted cords soared through the air. The weights whipped the cords around arms and legs, pulling the men to a stop as they tried to rise and flee. Then they turned with savage howls, snatched their clubs from their belts, and charged their attackers.

But the women had their swords ready as the wild men came at them. The swords stabbed and flickered in the air in darting flashes of light. One of the wild men howled and dropped his club, clutching at his stomach, where red blood was suddenly flowing over the filth-matted hair. In an instant the woman who had struck him closed with him, jerking the cord so that he toppled to the ground. As he went down, she shifted her grip on the sword and struck with the flat of the blade at his temple. There was a solid *smack*, and the heavy-muscled arms and legs relaxed.

The other three men had managed to avoid the women's initial rush. Now they had formed a rough triangle, back to back, waving their clubs and growling and cursing savagely at the women circling around them. The bare-breasted woman threw her head back and laughed harshly. The leader motioned her to silence with a sharp gesture of her spear.

Suddenly one of the wild men broke and ran. Blade noticed that he had a massive triangular blue scar on his stomach. The cord around his treelike thigh went tight as a bar with an audible *twung*. One of the women darted at him, but his club thrashed out at her, striking her sword aside with a clang. She jumped back as suddenly as she had moved in, rubbing a hand numbed by the shock. The wild man jerked again on the cord, making the woman holding it stagger and nearly lose her balance. The man's eyes widened as he saw that. Waving his club high over his head, he threw it straight at the woman. It struck her on the side of the jaw, and Blade heard the crunch of breaking bone. The woman gave a muffled scream of pain and let go the cord.

Instantly the wild man leaped high into the air, six feet off the ground. He sailed over the heads of the circle of women with a scream of triumph. Two waved swords frantically upward, one grabbed desperately for her bow, the leader came rushing over with her spear held ready. But before any of them could close, the scarred wild man was vanishing into the forest. Branches and twigs crackled behind him in a rapidly diminishing uproar. Blade could not help hoping the fugitive would get away.

With one comrade down and the other fled, the remaining two wild men seemed to have no will left to resist. With pathetically childlike whimpers, they threw their clubs down and slumped to the ground, their heads hanging low. The seven women still uninjured closed in and slashed the men's belts. They did not seem to care much whether they nicked the flesh underneath or not. Blade saw one of the men wince, and a bloody furrow appeared on his hairy skin just above his groin.

The leader of the women now barked a single sharp command. The bare-breasted woman ran back into the trees and vanished for a moment. When she came out, she was carrying an armful of metal stakes, short lengths of rope, and two of the small axes. With quick blows of the axes the women drove eight of the stakes into the ground. Then they spread-eagled the two men on their backs, tied by wrists and ankles to the stakes. Two of the women went to aid the one struck by the club, who was now sitting up, moaning and holding

27

her shattered and bloody jaw. There was an unmistakable tension, an air of something about to happen, in the clearing. Blade could almost smell it.

Now the leader stepped forward, moving with a sensuous, catlike grace. She stood nearly six feet tall. She stood over one of the spread-eagled men, raised her spear, then prodded him in the genitals with the butt. He arched his body and wriggled from side to side as much as the tight bindings at wrists and ankles would let him.

The leader let her spear fall, and drew off her gloves. Her hands went to the belt of her trousers, and undid the heavy brass buckle. Slowly she began to writhe her hips back and forth in a swaying motion, like a snake trying to charm a bird. Blade watched her face. He saw that she was trying to work herself up into a state of arousal—and before too long, it was obvious that she was succeeding. Occasionally she would clasp one or both hands over her breasts.

Suddenly she jerked off her tunic and stood bare to the waist above the wild man. Another jerk, and her trousers slid down her gracefully rounded thighs. Her stomach was as flat as a board, with only the faintest creases arrowing down toward the thick mass of curly hair between her thighs. The trousers slid all the way down to the ground, and she stepped out of them and kicked them carelessly off to one side. Blade shifted his gaze from her naked body to her face. Her eyes were wide and almost glazed, her mouth open, and her breathing so hard and fast that Blade could hear it clearly.

Blade was uncomfortably aware that the sight was arousing him. And it was doing the same to the men on the ground. Both now jutted up like miniature flagpoles and were writhing back and forth, gnashing their teeth and clawing at the earth with their fingers.

Suddenly the woman stepped forward until she was straddling the spread-eagled form of the first man. Then in a single, swift motion she plunged down onto him. She gave a great gasp as his rigid maleness vanished deep inside her. Then she began to rock back and forth, faster and faster, the gasps turning into moans and the moans into whimpers of delight. Her head went back until her hair came undone and flowed down her back. Blade could see her swollen, engorged nipples dark against the tanned flesh of her breasts.

Then a great shudder went through her, a second, a third. In the same moment the man on the ground cried out harshly in pleasure. The woman stayed where she was for another moment. Then slowly, staggering on legs that seemed barely able to support her, she stepped away from him. After only a few steps her legs gave up, and she sank down onto the needle-covered ground. Her head was down, and Blade could see her breasts heaving from her rapid breathing.

Now the bare-breasted woman was taking off her trousers, throwing her tunic aside, and walking over to the other man. She did not bother with the slow dance to arouse herself or the man. Apparently the sight of the first coupling had done all that she needed.

One by one, the seven uninjured women used the spread-eagled men, alternating between them. The eighth woman, the one with the broken jaw, was obviously feeling too sick to join in the proceedings, but Blade noticed that her trousers were unbuckled, and both her hands were down inside the waistband, moving vigorously. If this was a female-dominated society, sex with a man might well be a luxury item, like fine brandy or sports cars in Home Dimension. Blade grinned at the comparison. But whatever their sex life might be, these women looked tough and competent. They would be formidable opponents, offering few chances for mistakes.

Eventually both the capacities of the men and the lusts of the women were exhausted. Two of the women took axes and went off into the woods. A few minutes later they came back with stout poles, made from cut-down and trimmed saplings. The exhausted men were unbound, then swiftly slung from the poles and their wrists and ankles tied again. Blade saw the men wince

29

as the tightly bound cords cut into their flesh. After a few hours of this, they would be beyond either walking or defending themselves. If he wanted to rescue them, it would be a one-man show.

But did he want to rescue them? That they had been obscenely abused by the huntresses didn't change the fact that the wild men were hardly above the level of apes. If there was any civilization in this dimension—and Blade was beginning to wonder about that—it probably belonged to the huntresses. But they might be hard to approach. Certainly they would not welcome the release of their captives.

But, damn it, he was not going to simply sit here while the women carted those poor bastards off into the woods! At the very least, he was going to trail them until they made camp for the night. Then he could see what to do about the wild men, and only after that try to approach the women.

Blade looked up. The light coming through the gaps in the forest cover overhead was getting unmistakably dimmer and showing a reddish tinge. The day was moving on toward evening, and the women would be making camp soon. And they would not be marching very far before they made camp either, not carrying the wild men. They must weigh well over two hundred pounds apiece.

Blade settled down to wait as comfortably as he could. The insects were gone, but with the fading daylight it was getting chilly under the trees. The needles seemed to prick more than before, and the resins of the tree stuck to his bare skin like glue.

He did not have to wait very long, however. After binding the two men to the carrying poles, the women retrieved their clothing and gear. Then the leader pointed at four of her band. They paired off and each pair hoisted one of the carrying poles on their shoulders. Blade heard the wild men gasp at the strain put on their wrists and ankles. Then the leader took her position at the head of the line and brandished her

30

spear aloft. Slowly the huntresses marched off into the now fast-darkening forest.

Blade continued to cling to the branch for a good ten minutes more, until all sound of the marching women had faded away in the forest. Then he dropped lightly down to the ground, picked out their trail in the leaves and needles, and set off after them.

4

Blade could easily have trailed the women, even if they had been moving fast or trying to conceal their tracks. His survival training had been the best that England could offer—and his survival experience was even better, the result of sixteen trips into Dimension X.

But, as he had expected, the women moved slowly, encumbered by their prisoners and their wounded comrade. And they left a trail as visible as an elephant's. Apparently it had never occurred to the lithe huntresses that anything in the forest could turn the tables on them, make them the hunted. Probably they were right, in spite of that surprising display of craft and speed by the scarred wild man who had escaped. But Blade was not one of the wild men. The women were in for a considerable surprise when he slipped into their camp.

The women did not make camp until it was deep twilight, with the sky turning purple overhead and the stars already coming out. Apparently they had some sort of lamps—Blade could see yellow firefly glows through the trees as he lay under a bush, watching and waiting. Then the ruddy light of a large campfire spread through the trees. Blade heard cheerful voices, the clatter of weapons and cooking gear, and occasional dull chopping noises. It sounded as though they were cutting wood to keep the fire going through the night.

Gradually the noises died away, except for the crackling of the fire and a faint sizzling sound that

Blade could not identify. Probably the women had settled down to their evening meal. Blade decided to slip in closer and spy out the camp. He wanted to release the prisoners, not just blunder about in the darkness, tripping over roots and the sleeping bodies of the women.

As silent as a ghost, he slipped from one tree to another, and yet another. Each time he was a little closer to the fire's glow. Each time he stopped and waited, almost holding his breath, listening for any reaction from the camp to suggest that he might have been heard. But there was only the wind in the tree-tops high above, the crackle of the fire, and that sizzling. He continued his slow, stalking approach. In a few more minutes, he found a tree that gave him a clear view of the camp.

He saw then that he didn't need to worry any more about helping the wild men. They were beyond help. Parts of their bodies lay in a mangled and bloody heap under a bush. Other parts, stuck on long wooden poles, were turning slowly over the campfire. As the fat dripped off into the flames, it made the sizzling noise Blade had heard.

Blade recognized arms, legs, and various internal organs on the spits. Then he saw one of the women reach into the coals on the edge of the fire with a long stick and rake out a steaming, blackened head. A sharp blow with one of the axes, and the skull was opened. The woman motioned the leader over, and the leader squatted down and began rummaging around in the skull with her knife. Apparently the brains of the kill were the leader's right.

Then the wind shifted and brought to Blade's nose a powerful odor of roasting meat and burning fat. At that point he knew that he could not sit here watching the cannibal feast any longer. He turned and bolted for the safe, secure darkness. He was careless of noise, but the women behind him were too busy stuffing themselves to listen for noises in the darkness around them. Blade was able to get a good hundred yards from the camp before his outraged stomach finally gave up the struggle for self-control. There was not much in his stomach, for it had been a long time since his breakfast in Home Dimension. But it was also a long time before his stomach stopped heaving—a long time after there was anything in it to heave up. At the thought of having to deal with the cannibal huntresses as the highest civilization in this dimension, his stomach nearly revolted a second time.

But if he could not save the wild men, he could certainly make sure that the huntresses didn't get back home without at least the scare of their lives. Blade ran over his memories of the campsite. As careless as they seemed to be, they would still probably leave at least one woman on guard. But she might not be very alert. And after gorging themselves, the rest of the women would most likely be so fast asleep that a hand grenade tossed among them would not wake them. It should be fairly easy. But Blade still considered every possible pitfall and obstacle to his planned raid on the camp. When it still seemed like a good idea after that, he gave a small sigh of relief. Then he crept in carefully to where he could again see the camp clearly and settled down to wait.

Blade had to wait longer than he had expected, or found comfortable. Night settled down on the forest, and with it the night's chill and the night's own swarm of insects. In his nakedness, Blade found the chill very uncomfortable. He was exceptionally resistant to extremes of temperature and knew that the chill would not impair his fighting ability, but he didn't like it any better for that.

The insects were not as bad. Unlike the biting swarms of the day, the insects of the night merely whined endlessly around his head. They got into his eyes, they got into his ears, they got into his mouth and had to be spat out with half-muttered curses.

Nor were the insects the only wildlife on the move in the forest. Cracking branches and soft footfalls told of animals passing by. Occasionally Blade would see a red flash as eyes reflected the light of the campfire. He was not particularly bothered by this. He knew that he could outfight barehanded most of the wild animals he was likely to meet. But some would be too large. And there was always the possibility that one of the animals might attract the attention of the camp.

But the huntresses paid no attention to what might be happening in the forest around them. They stuffed themselves with more meat than Blade thought seven women could eat, taking their time at it. They also prepared a broth and spooned several bowls of it into their comrade with the broken jaw. Gradually the meat that had been roasting over the fire vanished, and white, shiny bones piled up. The bare-breasted woman had now pulled on her tunic against the night's chill. Blade saw her take the bones and crack them open with an axe, then pass around the pieces. As the women sucked out the marrow, Blade felt his stomach heaving again. But there was nothing left in it. After a while he got it back under control and continued to watch in grim silence, as motionless as a statue.

After they had eaten, the women drank and washed their greasy hands and faces with water from skin bags. They collected dry branches from all around their campsite and piled up the fire until it was a roaring orange pyramid shooting flames and sparks ten feet into the air. They dug into their sacks and pulled out heavy hide cloaks. Finally they pulled off their moccasins and tunics, wrapped themselves in the cloaks until they looked like giant sausages, and lay down to sleep.

As Blade had expected, the women left only one sentry on guard. It was the woman who had gone bare-breasted. She was fully armed, with bow, quiver, sword, and knife. Step by step, Blade began to work his way around the camp to a spot where he could take the guard from behind.

Each time he stopped, he looked at the camp. It was obvious that the woman's heart really wasn't in

35

her job. The first time Blade looked, she was energetically striding about the camp, hand on her sword hilt, eyes trying to look into the darkness in all directions at once. The second time he looked, she was standing still, but straight as a tree. The third time, her shoulders were drooping. The fourth time, she was squatting by the fire, balancing herself on her bow. The fifth time . . .

Moving without making a sound, Blade took nearly half an hour to get into position on the opposite side of the camp. By that time the woman had given up any effort to stay on her feet. She was sitting on the ground, legs crossed, bow laid across her knees, shoulders bowed, and head nodding. She was so obviously fighting to stay awake that Blade could hardly keep from laughing. All he had to do was wait until she dozed off, then move in. He would get no more resistance from the camp than he would get from eight newborn babies.

He waited a while longer, until he could be sure that the sentry was as deeply asleep as the other seven. The chill was beginning to numb his toes and fingers before he decided to move in. He stood up and worked them to get the blood flowing again. Then he began a slow, stalking approach, step by step, feeling his way forward. There was silence in the forest now, except for the whine of the insects and the occasional crackles of the dying fire. The eight women made no sound, not even a snore or a moan.

Closer and closer Blade crept. He grinned savagely when he saw that the women had carefully stacked their weapons in the center of their camp. Once he was between them and their weapons . . .

Two, three, four more steps, and he was at the edge of the clearing. Four more steps and he would be in striking range of the slumped-over sentry. He could have the whole camp at his mercy within seconds.

And knowing that made it impossible for him to kill. If the eight women had been coming at him with swords in their hands, he would not have held back

36

from killing them. Anyone who hesitates in such a situation doesn't live to be praised for his chivalry. But, as he had anticipated, the women were and would be as helpless as so many babies. It was hardly in Blade to cut the throats of eight sleeping men. It was beyond him to do the same to eight sleeping women, whatever their vices.

But there were other ways to deal with them that would make them think twice about their next hunting trip. Blade took those last four steps and came up behind the sentry. His hands flashed down like striking snakes, and his thumbs snapped shut on key nerves. The woman twitched once, then slumped even farther down, into an even deeper sleep.

Blade strode over to the pile of weapons. He picked up a sword and with it cut all the bowstrings, one by one. Then he threw the bows themselves on the fire. The arrows followed. The fire, which had been dying down, began to blaze up again in a great crackling and snapping. Blade began to pick up the swords and drop them also into the flames. The metal would not burn, but after a few minutes in the campfire it would have no temper left. The women might be able to use their swords for butter knives, but not for weapons.

He was picking up the fourth sword when one of the women threw off her cloak and sat up. Apparently the sudden flareup of the campfire had awakened her. Her eyes widened as she saw Blade's tall figure silhouetted against the fire. Then she gave a shriek of surprise and fury and hurled herself forward. Her hand dropped to her belt, and a knife flashed.

Blade could have spitted the woman like a barbecued chicken if he had wanted to. But he did not thrust with the sword as she rushed wildly at him. Instead, he brought it over and down, striking hard at her knife hand. He wanted to disarm her without hurting her, if possible.

But she was moving too fast for such precise aim. The sword ripped into her hand, and she gave another

37

kind of scream. She lost her balance, but her rush carried her forward, to sprawl at Blade's feet.

Instantly he slammed his right foot down on her left hand and aimed his sword at the back of her neck. Her screams had awakened the other women. They were sitting up now, staring at Blade. He reached down to pick up another sword and waved it at them. The firelight struck dazzling reflections from the polished steel.

"Don't move, any of you," he said. He did not raise his voice or show any anger. He might have been describing the weather. "If you do, she dies first." He jerked his head downward. "Then the rest of you. Just lie quietly, and you'll all live to get home—with luck."

"Who—you?" exclaimed one of the women, shaking her head as if trying to drive away a nightmare. Most of the others merely stared at Blade, as if they still could not believe that they were awake. But the leader's voice was calm when she spoke. Blade instantly marked her down as the most dangerous of the eight.

"You are not of the Senar, are you?" she said.

"The ones I saw you rape, kill, and eat? No, I am not of them."

"Then what are you doing in Brega, defying the Laws of Mother Kina? And how did you get into our camp without—?"

Blade grinned, but it was not a friendly grin. "I think it is not your time to ask questions, woman. But I will say this. I came into your camp as I did because your sentry was so glutted with Senar flesh that she fell asleep. A child could have done as much. And I am not a child. I am a warrior of my people."

"Your people—?"

"Are not your concern, woman. Perhaps the guard your party keeps is, though." The leader nodded, and shot a poisonous glare at the sleeping sentry. Blade could easily see that she would take out this night's humiliation on the sentry the next morning, slowly and painfully.

38

He waited until he thought the leader had savored that picture long enough. Then he said, "But I am taking your sentry with me. I should like some company as I travel through these lonely forests." His face twisted into a goatish leer. The leader winced, realizing what sort of "company" Blade had in mind. "She will live as long as I hear no sounds of pursuit behind me. Now, woman—throw me your tunic and trousers. And be quick about it." Blade reinforced his words by bringing his sword against the neck of the woman at his feet.

The leader had enough sense not to argue further. She stood up and threw her tunic at Blade. It landed at his feet. She undid her trousers and let them slide down her legs into a heap on the ground. Blade read in her eyes a moment's hope that the sight of her nudity would distract him. But he kept his face stone hard, and she gave an audible sigh and threw the trousers after the tunic. Blade bent without taking his eyes off the woman, scooped up both garments, then stepped back from the woman on the ground.

This was the dangerous moment. For a few seconds he would have no hostages to threaten. If the leader was willing to risk or even sacrifice her life, she could force Blade to concentrate on killing her. And then the other women would have their chance, if they could take it.

Either the leader was not willing, or she judged that her followers would not take any chance she might give them. She remained motionless, glaring at Blade, as he stepped over to the sleeping sentry. He bent down and one massive arm scooped her up as easily as a child. He threw her over his shoulder, then stepped back farther, outside the circle.

"Remember," he said quietly. "She lives as long as you don't follow me. You pursue, and she dies. And then the rest of you. One by one."

He turned his back contemptuously on the women and was gone into the darkness of the forest.

5

Blade had done his best to leave the women no equipment for anything except a hasty retreat from the forest, and therefore no alternative. And he hoped that the threat to kill his prisoners would keep them from sending any other hunting parties after him.

Once out of sight of the campfire, he stopped long enough to pull on the clothes and buckle on the various weapons. As he had expected, the tunic and trousers were a snug fit. But they were less uncomfortable than running around the forest with the chilly breezes working on his bare skin. And the weapons would enable him not only to defend himself, but also to hunt down the food he and his prisoner would need to keep them alive until—

Until what? As he finished dressing, Blade realized that for once he had no very clear idea of what to do or where to go. This land, it seemed, was called Brega. The wild men were called—at least by the huntresses—the Senar. The huntresses seemed to prey successfully on the Senar, using them for sport, sex, and food. But Blade had no idea how many of the hunting parties or of the Senar might be in the forest that stretched for some unknown number of miles around him. And he had even less idea of what might lie beyond the forest.

Blade shrugged and realized that he could not answer any such questions now. He would have to talk to his prisoner before he could hope to understand the way things were in Brega. He bent down and once more hoisted the woman over his shoulder. Then he strode away into the night.

He kept on the move until dawn began turning the sky high above from black to blue to gray to pale pink. The breeze died away, and the birds began to whistle and chirp in the trees overhead. Although his mouth was turning dry, Blade kept on for another hour, until it was broad daylight. At that point he came to a small stream, bubbling out from a mossy patch under a bush. This seemed as good a stopping point as any and better than most. Gently he lowered the woman to the ground, almost gasping at the relief to his half-numb shoulder. The woman was small and comparatively light, but there is no really light weight for carrying seven miles through a dark forest on one shoulder.

As the woman touched the ground, her eyes opened and her breathing quickened. But she made no effort to rise or even move. Blade took off his tunic, soaked one sleeve in the spring, and mopped her face with it. Then he rummaged in her pack until he found a small tin cup, filled it with water, and gave it to her. She practically snatched the cup from his hands, spilling half the water in the process. She gulped the rest thirstily, like an animal, without taking her eyes off Blade. He saw there was stark animal terror in those eyes, and almost by reflex his hand moved toward the hilt of his sword. The girl looked ready to risk almost anything to get away—or failing that, to kill him.

He would have liked to stay here long enough to find some way of reassuring the girl. But he still wasn't sure that they were safe from meeting other parties of huntresses or other parties of Senar. Blade didn't care to risk a fight with the huntresses, and he did not really want to fight the unfortunate wild men. The Senar seemed to have enough troubles of their own without his adding to them.

So he once more dug into the pack and pulled out one of the weighted throwing lines. Cutting it into pieces with his knife, he tied the girl's hands behind her. Then he tied the other, longer piece around her neck.

41

Finally he packed up all the loose gear and hauled the girl to her feet.

"We must go on," he said. Blade spoke slowly and carefully, without raising his voice, as he might have spoken to a frightened child. He did not trust the girl yet, nor would he do so for quite a while. But he wanted to get it across to her that he was not going to treat her the way the Senar no doubt treated captured women. The terror in the girl's eyes told him how vicious that treatment must be.

"We must go on," he repeated, in the same tone. "I do not want to meet any more of the women of Brega for a long time. But I am not of the Senar. So I do not want to meet them either. You should not try to run away. If you do, you might meet the Senar. If you did, you would have nothing to fight them with. And I would not be there to kill them and save you. I am a hunter in my own lands, and I can use bow and sword. I will protect you from the Senar, I promise you, as long as you stay with me."

At this point the girl burst into half-hysterical sobbing and dropped to her knees in front of Blade. When her sobbing had subsided to faint whimpering, she was able to choke out, "Thank you, for Mother Kina. Thank you, for Mother Kina. You are not of the Senar, not of the Senar."

"No, I am not of the Senar," Blade repeated firmly. "And I will not let them catch you or harm you. Now stand up, and let us go away from here, before the Senar find us."

Those last words made the girl spring up as if she had been stung by bees. Blade grabbed the end of the rope around her neck and wound the last foot of it around his hand. Then he nodded, and the girl stepped out to the full length of the rope and turned away into the trees.

However careless they might be, the huntresses of Brega were certainly in good condition. The girl kept pace with Blade almost every foot of the day's travel, with no sign of effort or strain except for a

42

sheen of sweat on her tanned skin. Blade kept them going all day, with stops every two hours or so for rest and water. He took advantage of one of those stops to shoot two large black squirrel-like beasts that incautiously peered down on him from a branch above.

They had to keep going for nearly an hour longer than Blade had intended in order to reach water. It was nearly dark when they found a small, rushing stream and Blade indicated they would make camp for the night. The girl looked as though she could have gone on for several more hours. But the muscles of Blade's legs were beginning to develop hard and painful knots. He sat down with a sigh of relief.

After a few minutes' rest he rose, tethered the girl to a branch, and began collecting firewood. The bank of the stream was littered with dry needles and windfallen branches, and it did not take him long. A few sparks from the flint lighter in the pack, and the needles flared into crackling orange flames. When the fire was going well, Blade pulled out the two giant squirrels and began skinning and gutting them.

The girl watched him intently, never taking her eyes off the fast-moving knife. Poor girl, thought Blade. She's still wondering if I'm going to start on her with the knife after I finish the squirrels.

Blade finished the first squirrel, thrust it onto a stick, and braced the stick over the fire. Then he took the knife and stepped over to the girl. She turned pale under her tan, and a cold sweat of stark terror broke out all over her.

"Would you like to cut up the other one?" he asked.

The girl jumped as though Blade had actually stabbed her, and stared up at him, eyes wide open.

"Hold up your hands," said Blade, firmly but quietly. Numbly, the girl obeyed. With two quick slashes, Blade sliced through the cords binding her wrists. She gave a little gasp of surprise and held her hands up in front of her, staring at them as though she had

43

never seen them before. She wiggled her half-numb fingers, whimpering at the pain of circulation returning to them.

"Would you like to cut up the other animal?" Blade repeated. Then he took the knife by the point and laid it down on the ground, hilt facing the girl. At the same time he stepped back until he was outside easy stabbing range. He would trust the girl only up to a point.

Slowly and tentatively the girl reached out for the knife until her fingers caressed the bone hilt. Senar bone? Blade wondered. "Yes," he said. "You may take it. I think you know how to use it."

There was a grunt from the girl that might have been the word "Yes." Then her hand clutched the knife and snatched it up from the ground. She held it stiffly at arm's length for a moment. Blade watched her carefully, ready to snatch it back from her if she made any move to use it on him—or on herself. Then slowly her other hand reached out for the squirrel, caught it by the tail, and dragged it to within reach of the knife. Blade could not keep back a sigh of relief. The woman heard it, looked up at him again, and managed a weak smile. Then she bent down and went to work on the squirrel.

The squirrel meat was tough and gamy, but it was juicy and there was plenty of it. Blade and the girl each finished off one of the squirrels, then washed their hands and faces in the stream. After that Blade piled more wood on the fire and sat down cross-legged on the needles. Once again, he was careful to sit far enough away from the girl that she would have no chance for a sudden attack.

"Now," he said cheerfully. "What is your name? I cannot go on calling you 'woman' for all the time that we will be together in this forest."

The girl's upper teeth sank into her lower lip for a moment. Then she said, "My name is Wyala."

"Wyala." Blade rolled the name around on his tongue for much longer than was really necessary.

44

Then he said, "My name is Blade. I have traveled into Brega from a distant land."

"That I can see—now," said Wyala. "You are not of the Senar. They are all hairy and thick in their bodies. And when they capture a woman of the city, they—" She was unable to finish the sentence, but she didn't need to. The expression on her face told Blade enough.

"Yes, I saw the Senar that your band captured," said Blade. "And I saw all the things you did to them." Wyala started. "Yes. I was hiding in a tree above the clearing where you fought and captured the Senar. I saw what you did to them." Wyala's face puckered up as though she were going to cry again and slowly turned bright red. Blade sat in silence, letting Wyala stew in her own embarrassment.

Finally the girl raised her head and stared at Blade almost defiantly. "Why should we not treat the Senar so? They are enemies to all who follow the Law of Mother Kina."

"Do you treat the men of the city of Brega that way also?" asked Blade. He could not quite keep the sarcasm out of his voice.

"The men of the city?" Wyala looked confused for a moment. "Oh—the breeding males. No, we do not treat them so. Why should we? They are shut up in the House of Fertility and only the guardians ever see them. And a guardian who mistreated one of her charges would be cast down from her post, perhaps even sentenced to the arena. But no guardian would ever do anything like that. They are sworn to Mother Kina by an oath much stronger than the hunters take. *We* can treat the Senar as we choose." The note of defiance was back in her voice.

"So I see," said Blade. He saw a good deal more than he was willing to admit to Wyala. As he had suspected, he was in a dimension of women. Or at least one ruled by women, where the only civilized males were the breeding males in the House of Fertility in the city. He frowned. Communication with anybody in

45

this dimension was going to be difficult, he suspected. The Senar were below the level of savages and would have the savage's belief that the stranger was an enemy. The women of the city—the worshipers of Mother Kina—were a good deal more civilized. But they would be almost as likely as the Senar to shoot first and ask questions afterwards. Their religion would require it, at least if the stranger was a man. There were times, Blade realized, when a woman companion might be more useful than another man. He made a mental note to mention the point when and if he returned to Home Dimension.

But for the moment he was alone in the woman-ruled dimension of Brega, and he would have to make his way through it as best he could. He had done it well enough sixteen times before. Barring extraordinary ill luck, he could see no reason for not doing so a seventeenth time. And, he reflected wearily, an eighteenth, and nineteenth, and so on and on until his luck ran out or they finally found someone else to go—man, woman, child, chimpanzee, or whatever!

He looked at Wyala. "I should like to travel to the city and speak with those who follow the Law of Mother Kina. Although men rule in my own country, we respect the gods of others." Blade smiled in grim amusement at his own remark. At this rate, he should have enough practice at pandering to local prejudices to run for Parliament when he retired!

Wyala's mouth dropped open. "Men rule? How can that be? The Law of Mother Kina is that it cannot be so. It cannot. Men are filled with the killing madness that brought on the disaster to end the old days of Brega. The disaster purged them from the world, and Mother Kina now rules."

"Nonetheless, it is otherwise in my homeland," said Blade. "Perhaps your men were different. But in my homeland the men have no madness in them, at least no more than the women. The disaster has not yet come, and both men and women would laugh at the Law of Mother Kina."

"No," said Wyala again. "No, no, *no*." The last word was almost a scream. "Women—at the mercy of men—men thinking, speaking reasoned words—no," she whimpered.

"Yes," said Blade quietly. "It is so. And what is this nonsense about women 'at the mercy of men'? Why do you think they cannot both be thinking beings together? And even if men have women at their mercy —well, what of it? I had all eight of your band at my mercy last night. I could have snapped the necks and cut the throats of every last one of you and left you for the worms and the ants to strip to bare bones. And I could have used any or all of you for my pleasure, until I had had enough. But I did none of those things.

"And after I took you away I could have mistreated you even more easily. But I did not. All I did was tie you so that you could not escape or try to kill me. I saw that you were a fighting woman, and might do these things."

Slowly, Wyala nodded. "Perhaps I believe you. But I do not know if the women of the city will believe you. If you go to the city, you will be killed before you even see its walls. I do not care how good a warrior you are. And"— she swallowed— "they will kill me also if I come with you."

"Perhaps all you say is true," said Blade sharply. "But what else are we supposed to do? Certainly we cannot go to the Senar. They would probably kill me just as fast as the women of the city would. They would certainly kill you, and do others things as well, since I could not protect you from hundreds of the Senar."

"I know," said Wyala miserably. "But—to take a wild man who is not a wild man—to the city itself— they would not believe that such a thing as you are exists. They would think that you were one of the Senar in disguise, trying to get into the city so that you could run wild and kill and rape. And they would not listen to me long enough to save us. They wouldn't,

47

they wouldn't, they wouldn't!" She was crying now, in frustration and despair at not being able to make Blade believe her.

There was no point in continuing the argument tonight. Blade sighed and moved over to sit beside Wyala, putting an arm around her heaving shoulders. At first the unaccustomed touch of a man's heavily muscled body made her start and stiffen. But after a minute or two she realized that there was no danger in Blade's touch. Her own arm went around his waist, and her head slipped down onto his shoulder. After a few minutes more, she was snuggling up against him as naturally as any girl of Home Dimension.

Wyala was warm and comfortable against Blade, but darkness had fallen now and it was getting chilly. He began to think of suggesting that they wrap themselves up in their cloaks and get some sleep. There would be another long day's travel tomorrow, wherever they decided to go.

Then Blade became aware that Wyala's free hand was reaching out to him. He had stripped off his tunic before dinner, and now her small fingers were fumbling their way over his bare skin. He could feel them twining the hair on his chest and pressing against the hard muscles of his stomach. They were not very expert fingers, but they were warm and gentle in their movements. Unmistakably, Blade began to feel the beginnings of arousal.

He did not move or speak. He was not at all sure Wyala knew what she was doing or where it might lead. He wanted to be sure. So he waited, and felt the fingers creep down across his stomach, and still lower. She made no effort to unlace the front of his trousers. But when she felt a swelling bulge under her fingers, she seemed to recognize it for what it was. Her fingers did not move away. Instead, they stayed and stroked and played. Blade began to find it harder and harder to stay motionless. His breathing began to quicken.

His arousal increased further, and now it was impossible to doubt that Wyala knew what she was doing and was doing it on purpose. Why didn't really matter—and Blade didn't really care.

Now his own arms went around Wyala from behind, cupping both her breasts. Even under the heavy fabric of her tunic their firm, full curves were exciting. His fingers tugged at the lacings of her tunic until its front gaped partway open, then slipped inside to play on her bare skin. Now she was aware of his hands moving on her, but said nothing. She twisted her body to give his hands more freedom to move and gave a little gasp as one finger curled around a nipple. The nipple promptly sprang to life, swelling up into a hard little nubbin that pressed against Blade's fingers. He cupped both breasts in his hands and heard her gasp more loudly. If Wyala was not an excited woman now, Blade had never seen one in his life.

Her fingers had stopped their work on his trousers as he began his on her breasts. But Wyala's excitement kept Blade's alive. He finished undoing the laces of her tunic and slipped it off her shoulders. She helped him get it the rest of the way off, then turned toward him, bare to the waist. Seen close up, Wyala's breasts were indeed full, a woman's breasts rather than a girl's, but a young woman. There was no sag or slump in the magnificent curves. The large, dark nipples stood up proud and high. Wyala arched her back to thrust her breasts almost into Blade's face, and he lowered his lips to brush her skin. He felt warmth and smelled good health in that skin.

As Blade's lips moved up and down Wyala's body, her hands went back to work on his trousers. Excitement rose in him again. It rose higher as Wyala undid the lacing of the trousers and unbuckled the belt. Her hands plunged down into Blade's groin as though she was plunging them into a basket of fruit. They still weren't very skilled hands, but what they lacked in skill they made up for in vigor.

Wyala pulled herself partly out of his arms and bent her own lips to run across Blade's skin. Those lips were warm and wet, and as they crept lower and lower on his body, Blade groaned. His hands reached out for her again, ran down the smooth skin of her back, and slipped down into her trousers. Her buttocks were as firm and sweetly rounded as her breasts. And when he moved his hands around to her groin, he found the thick tangle of hair there already dampening with her mounting passion.

Wyala seemed to take Blade's hands moving on her as a signal. With a graceful twisting of her body, she stood up and wriggled out of her trousers. One kick and they went flying across the clearing, nearly landing in the campfire. Both Blade and Wyala laughed out loud. Then Blade was also on his feet. But he had no chance to pull down his trousers. Wyala's hands clutched at them, dragging them down. As her hands worked on the trousers, they also stroked the inside of Blade's thighs and his massive, swollen organ. And where her hands went, a moment later her lips followed. Blade groaned again and wondered if Wyala knew how little of this men could really take. His own endurance was enormous, but there was such a thing as too much even for him.

But before they reached that point, Wyala took the initiative again. Snatching up the fallen trousers and tunics, she spread them on the ground, then lay back on them. She did not say anything coherent. By now she probably couldn't. But the expression on her face and her gasping breath and murmurs made it obvious that the time had come for her. Blade knelt down at her feet, gently pulled her legs apart, then moved forward, down—and in.

Wyala's face took on an unmistakable look of surprise as Blade slipped inside her. Even in his excitement, Blade remembered that the male organs of the Senar had been grotesquely lumpish and hairy. A normal set of male genitals inside her might be a novelty.

If there was any novelty, it certainly wasn't affecting Wyala's responses. Blade began with an unusual effort to go slowly, to make Wyala's introduction to normal sex as gentle as possible. He soon realized that he had no need to do anything of the kind. Wyala was almost sopping wet inside, and she locked arms and legs around him as if she wanted to drag him into her or flatten herself against him. Her hips writhed and wriggled in a steadily increasing tempo, jerking upward against him faster and faster.

Then in one explosive moment her hips increased their movements until they were almost vibrating. Her arms and legs tightened around Blade until he could hardly breathe, and her nails dug into his back until he felt as though he was being whipped. Her mouth opened and shut like a dying woman's, but nothing came out of it except gasps and little hisses. Blade felt her pelvic muscles jerking under his groin and her wet canal tightening around his own erection.

That tightening was all he needed to overcome the last bit of his self-control. All the built-up pressure came jetting out hotly into Wyala, and went on jetting.

Eventually both Blade and Wyala exhausted the last of their passion. Blade managed to find the energy to roll off the girl and lie down on the clothes beside her. They lay there motionless and silent for a few minutes. Then Blade found a little more energy, got up, and picked up the cloaks. He laid both on top of Wyala, then lay down again and crept in under them. Now that the burning heat of their common passion had vanished, the night's cold struck unpleasantly at their bare skins.

After a few minutes, Wyala stirred. She lay for a time staring at Blade. Then she rolled over against him, her body warm, soft, and comfortable against his. He put his arms around her, for her pleasure and for his.

"You are *not* of the Senar," she said. The tone of voice was that of someone who has no more doubts.

51

"And you—you are not like a woman who has lived only among women," said Blade with a grin. He had no doubts on that either.

Soon they drifted off to sleep in each other's arms.

6

Blade had been awake and on the move for almost thirty-six hours, so it was well after dawn when he awoke. This was an unpleasant surprise. Blade was a man who believed that half of beating one's opponent was getting up before him in the morning.

However, there wasn't much point in moving early until he and Wyala had decided where they were going. He raised that point after a breakfast of water and the cold remains of the squirrels.

Wyala seemed more rational this morning than she had been the day before. Now she seemed to be used to the idea of there being a third kind of male in the world besides the breeding males and the Senar. She even seemed to be enjoying the discovery.

But she was just as stubborn as before on the point that Blade's approaching the city of Brega would be nothing but suicide for both of them. "How can you expect it to be otherwise, when we have known nothing but the Senar and the breeding males?"

"You yourself said that I do not look like either one."

"I know. And that is true. But how many of our hunters or warriors would see that—at least before they had killed you?"

"Have you nothing in the city but hunters and warriors?"

"Oh, no; we have many kinds of women. There are the governors, the guardians of fertility—" she listed a dozen more. "And they are chosen for their wisdom, so they might let you live a little while. But the hunters and the warriors will see you first and kill you before the higher wisdom groups can ever get a chance to see you."

"Perhaps. But suppose you came with me to the city? Could you not do something to convince the hunters and warriors that I should not be killed?"

Wyala cocked her head to one side as she considered that. Last night the idea had sent her virtually into hysterics. Today it merely seemed something to think over carefully before saying anything. This was a young woman of much common sense. Blade hoped very much that she would help him in his exploration of this dimension. He could hardly have found a better ally if he had ordered one specially in advance.

Finally she nodded. "It will be almost as much a risk for me as for you. They will think that you have captured me and forced me into cooperating with you by threats or torture. So they may kill you anyway—and then kill me afterwards." She hesitated. "But I will go with you if you want to go to the city. Could you possibly not go to the city at all? That would be safer for both of us."

Blade had to admit that the idea was more than usually tempting. The city of Brega sounded like a place of great danger for small rewards. However, duty was duty, until the day his luck ran out or they found someone new to take his place in the computer's chair. And Wyala was not only risking her life; she was risking it against everything she had been taught to believe in. There was high courage in her.

Blade bent over and kissed Wyala firmly on the lips. "Thank you for this. You are very brave, as well as very beautiful." Wyala smiled and blushed, then began busying herself with picking up the equipment and putting out the campfire.

Within a few minutes both had their gear loaded on their backs. The last thing Blade picked up was the remains of the cords he had used to tie Wyala the day before. He held them up in front of her and waved them around, laughing. She laughed too. Then with a flick of his wrist Blade tossed the cords into the stream. He stood and watched for a moment as they drifted out of sight. Then he turned back to Wyala.

"Let's go. Which way is the city?"

Wyala looked up at the blue sky for a moment, shading her eyes against the bright morning sun. "That way," she said finally, pointing. "Toward the sunrise."

"Good." Blade turned to the east, shifted his bow on his shoulder so that it rode more comfortably, and led the way into the trees.

Heading east meant virtually retracing their steps. This would mean traveling through well-watered country, which was fine with Blade. But it also meant a greater risk of encountering hunting parties from the city. Blade wished he had thought of picking up a set of weapons for Wyala during his raid on the camp. But how could he have known then that he would be able to treat her as a friend and ally, instead of merely keeping her as a prisoner?

They kept moving without a pause until nearly noon. They broke their journey then for a meal of bright yellow berries from a clump of bushes beside a small pool. They also refilled their water bottles.

Blade was kneeling by the stream, hooking his filled water bottle to his belt, when he suddenly heard Wyala scream in terror. He spun around, his hand dropping to his sword and snatching it clear of the scabbard in a single motion.

One of the Senar had burst out of the bushes by the pond, waving a massive branch instead of a club. He stopped and let out a shriek of rage and defiance as he saw Blade and the drawn sword. He drew his lips back from yellow-stained teeth in a savage snarl. Then Blade saw the great blue triangular scar on the Senar's stomach, and recognized him. This was the one who had found the speed and wit to escape from the hunting party that had taken his companions. And

55

that meant he was a considerably more dangerous opponent than the average Senar.

With his sword Blade motioned Wyala to get behind him. He wanted to get her out of reach of a quick grab by the man-creature so he could fight without having to worry about her. Wyala nodded and took two steps backward.

That brought another growl from the Senar. Wyala froze, looking in growing fear from Blade to the Senar and back to Blade. To Blade's surprise, the next noise from the Senar was three clearly recognizable words.

"*No*—Hairless One." The Senar brandished the club, then continued. "Not mountains here. Hairless Ones not keep women here. Nugun take."

"You will *not* take this woman," said Blade sharply. He raised the sword.

The Senar spat on the ground. "You—all Hairless Ones—weak. Fight with sharp sticks—not like Senar." The man-creature raised both his massively muscled arms and growled angrily.

Wyala gave a little gasp and took two more steps backward. "For the love of Mother Kina, kill it!" she gasped. "Don't just stand there. Kill it!" She drew her knife and held it out in front of her.

Wyala's words and movements nearly provoked a rush by the Senar. Blade took two steps forward and drew his own knife, holding it by the point, ready for throwing. It was badly balanced for that, but the Senar would be a big target and even a non-fatal wound should slow it down somewhat. At the same time he snapped, "Shut up!" to Wyala, without taking his eyes off—was Nugun the Senar's personal name?

Blade decided to assume it was. "Nugun!" he said, in the most commanding voice he could manage. The Senar started and raised his shaggy head. Enormous brown eyes stared hard into Blade's. There was more intelligence in them than Blade had expected.

"Nugun," he repeated more quietly. "You want this

woman?" He pointed at Wyala, who cringed and stared at him horror-stricken.

"Yes," said Nugun. "Hairless Ones in mountains get all good women. Senar get old ones, sick ones, ugly ones. This one—good woman." He jerked a hairy, black-nailed thumb at Wyala.

"Yes. She is a good woman. But she is *my* woman. I will not give her up without a fight with you."

"Hairless Ones not fight. Kill Senar with sharp sticks, throw sticks—kill Senar like animals." Nugun spat again.

"I will fight you, Nugun," said Blade. "And I will fight you with no sticks. Only with these." He raised his own arms over his head, and flexed his own massive muscles.

Nugun stared. Wyala gave a gasp of pure horror and started to lunge at Nugun. Blade shouted to the Senar, "Don't move!" then grabbed Wyala by the hair, hooked her ankles out from under her, and knocked her to the ground. She writhed and mewled for a moment, then quieted.

Blade bent down until he could whisper into her ear, "Damn it, Wyala! If you can't keep calm, I'll have to tie you up again. I want to be able to talk with this Senar, not just kill him."

"You're mad, Blade!" she gasped. "You can't talk with a Senar or trust him. He'll kill you if you fight him barehanded. They're all strong like animals. And then what will happen to me? What will happen to me?" The hysteria was back in her voice. Blade wished he had time to explain what he had in mind, but he knew that Nugun would grow impatient if he tried. And then he would have to kill the Senar, which was the last thing he wanted to do.

"Nugun won't kill me," he whispered quickly. "Even if he does, you can outrun him by the time he gets through fighting me. And you can keep your knife. But don't run away until you see how the fight is going. If you don't promise that, I'll have to tie you up again. Do you promise?"

"Yes." It was muffled and reluctant, but unmistakable.

"Good."

Blade stood up, threw his sword to the ground, then began unbuckling his belt. Nugun stared wide-eyed at him.

"You fight Nugun? No sticks?"

"No sticks, Nugun. I do not lie."

"Hairless Ones always lie."

"I do not, Nugun. I do not know what these other Hairless Ones do, but I do not lie."

"Maybe not. But you fight me."

"I fight you."

Blade had now stripped himself of all his weapons. Then he kicked off his boots and stripped off his tunic. He didn't want to take any chances with this fight. The Senar was well over six feet tall and must weigh close to three hundred pounds. Blade knew he would have the edge in unarmed-combat training and quick thinking. He would probably have the edge in speed. But his plan depended not only on defeating Nugun, but on defeating him without killing or even seriously hurting him. This was a far more difficult and dangerous thing to try against an unknown opponent.

Now Blade pointed at Nugun's improvised club. The Senar nodded, growled agreement, and threw the branch far away from him. He crouched down, rubbing the palms of his splay-fingered hands on the ground. His eyes glared into Blade's and a low growl sounded in his throat. Then suddenly he straightened up with a leap and charged at Blade.

Blade leaped aside from the rush with split seconds to spare. Nugun's ragged nails whistled down past his shoulder, only inches away. For all the Senar's bulk and thick legs, he was faster than Blade had expected. Now to find out just exactly how much faster. Blade had to know that before he could know what he could and could not try against this opponent.

Again Nugun made a rush, but this time Blade was clear in plenty of time. He swung around to Nugun's right, but the other spun in a blur of motion and struck out with one clublike arm. Blade ducked his head, but not quite quickly enough. The blow rode up over his shoulder and smashed against his left temple.

For a moment Blade was half-stunned, barely able to keep on his feet. Through stars and fireworks swirling in front of his eyes, he saw Nugun rushing in again. By reflex and desperation, he launched a kick at Nugun's right kneecap. The kick connected, with a jar that ran up Blade's leg into his body and made his teeth rattle. It was like kicking a granite block.

But the kick stopped Nugun as his hands were already reaching out for Blade's throat. With a growl of surprise and pain the Senar backed away, favoring his right leg. Blade noticed that and his thoughts were grim. That kick would have smashed the kneecap of a normal human opponent into a dozen pieces. But it had barely slowed Nugun. This was going to be a long fight, with victory going to the one who could give out the most punishment while taking the least. And Blade wasn't sure that would be him. Nugun was enormously tough—and if those hands of his ever got a good hold on Blade, the fight would be over then and there.

For the next few minutes, Blade concentrated on staying out of Nugun's range. He didn't care what the Senar thought of him for doing that. He could not afford to let Nugun get in a solid blow. Blade knew that he had been lucky the first time. He might not be so lucky a second time.

So he led Nugun a dance up and down the bank of the stream and around and around the bushes. He bobbed and wove; he ducked Nugun's punches and leaped aside from his rushes; he jeered and taunted him. Sometimes he pretended to close, but he always sprang back in time for Nugun's hands to close on nothing but empty air.

Nugun had no more fighting style than a six-year-old boy. All he knew was bull-like rushes, clublike

59

swings of his arms, and clutches with his long-nailed fingers. But his speed and strength made even these crude tactics dangerous.

After the first few minutes, Blade began moving in again, using all his training and speed to aim and deliver disabling blows. Now he aimed at a knee again, now at a shoulder, now at Nugun's hairy groin. Each time the blow went home. And each time Nugun merely grunted or snarled and clawed or swung furiously at Blade. Once his long nails raked across Blade's chest, leaving five red, oozing lines. At that the Senar threw back his head and howled in triumph, giving Blade just enough time to get out of range.

Any of Blade's blows would have crippled or at least fatally slowed any other opponent. But Nugun had an altogether inhuman capacity to take punishment. Reluctantly, Blade admitted to himself that it would be suicidal to try closing with Nugun until the man was slowed down a good deal more. If he could be, that is. Blade opened the distance between himself and the Senar, and the endless dance began again.

This time Blade had no idea how long it lasted. Minutes followed one another and seemed to stretch into hours. There was an iron band around his chest, white-hot gravel in his throat, knives stabbing into his leg muscles as he moved, rivers of sweat pouring off him, making his eyes sting. His only consolation was that sweat was also pouring off Nugun's body, and the other's eyes were beginning to dull with fatigue.

More minutes. With his breath rasping in his throat, Nugun snarled, "Hairless Ones not fight. I know. You give me woman."

"I am fighting, Nugun," said Blade sharply. "If you try to take the woman, I will use the sharp stick on you." Nugun's lips curled back from his teeth again, but he made no move toward Wyala. The woman was crouched behind a tree, knife in her hand, staring with wide, terror-stricken eyes at the battle raging by the stream.

Still more minutes. Blade began to wonder if Nugun's endurance would be greater than his own. At this rate, the fight would end with him sprawled flat on the ground, for Nugun to pick up and break in two like a stick over one knobby knee.

But now Nugun seemed to think that Blade was weakening. The Senar crouched, arms spread wide and hands curved into claws. Then he sprang forward out of the crouch, arms reaching low as if he wanted to grab Blade's legs and jerk him off his feet.

Behind him Blade heard Wyala scream out loud. But as Nugun's hands lunged for him, Blade was already leaping high. The clutching hands closed on empty air. For a moment Nugun was off balance, unable to bring his arms up to defend himself as he had always done before.

In that moment, Blade's attack struck home. Pivoting on one foot, he drove the heel of the other into Nugun's jaw. Again the solid jar shook every bone in Blade's body. But this time it also shook Nugun just as badly. The Senar's head jerked back and he snapped himself upright.

As he did, Blade completed the pivot, ducked, and came in under Nugun's guard. For a moment he was under the reach of those terrible arms, with a clear shot at Nugun's middle. Blade's balled fists drove into the hairy stomach, in a one-two punch that made a noise like a cannon shot. Once more Blade was jarred to the fillings in his teeth. Punching Nugun's stomach was like punching a bag of solid, wet sand. But Blade's knuckles still sank in, and all the breath *whooshed* out of his opponent in one foul-smelling gust.

There were a dozen or more things Blade could have done in the next second. But most of them were intended to kill an opponent—break his neck, crush his ribcage, tear his internal organs apart—or at least cripple him for life. Blade still did not want to do that to Nugun. In fact, he now wanted to do it even less than at the beginning of the fight. Nugun had been a brave opponent as well as a tough one.

So he ignored the risks of being close to Nugun if the man recovered his strength. As Nugun reeled, gasping for air, Blade grabbed the Senar's left arm and spun him around. It was like spinning around a stone statue, and Blade's own arms nearly popped out of their sockets with the strain. When he had Nugun turned around, Blade brought one foot up and scythed it hard across the back of Nugun's knees. Nugun reeled again, gave a savage growl of fear and despair, and this time he went down onto the ground, face forward.

Before Nugun could move or growl again, Blade had landed on his back and snatched one arm. He held that arm firmly, barely twisting it, while he poised his other hand over the back of Nugun's neck. No matter how thick that neck was, a strong blow there would certainly end Nugun's fighting days forever, and perhaps his life as well.

Blade bent lower and hissed in one hairy ear, "Don't move, Nugun. I can kill you any time I want to."

"Then kill," growled Nugun. "You not like Hairless Ones. You fight like Senar. You fight good. Nugun—weak. You kill now."

"I don't want to kill you," said Blade quietly. "I want you to live, and be my friend."

Nugun was silent for so long that Blade thought the man must have fainted. Then he said slowly, "Not kill?"

"No. Why should I?"

That was apparently a question beyond Nugun's mental resources. He was silent again until Blade asked him, "Remember the woman?"

"Yes. Nugun—did want."

"You don't want her now?"

"She—your woman. You stronger than Nugun."

"Yes. I am stronger than you are. And she is my woman. But will you be my friend?"

Hesitation, and more silence. Then, "Nugun is friend to new Hairless One. Nugun die for new Hairless One who not kill."

Blade stood up and backed away from the prostrate Senar. With a groan, Nugun shook himself and stood up. Blade thrust out a hand. After a moment's more hesitation, Nugun realized what the gesture meant. He took Blade's hand, and they shook vigorously.

When they were through shaking hands, Blade turned and went over to where he and Wyala had left their gear. As he did, he noticed that Wyala was gone. He swore.

"Hurt you, friend?" said Nugun.

Blade shook his head. "No. My woman has run away; that is all."

Nugun growled and shook his head angrily. "You go after her, beat when find her?"

"No," said Blade. "She must have thought you were going to kill me and did not trust you." Nugun looked hurt. Blade shrugged. "No doubt she'll be back when she realizes that you and I are friends now." He poured a cup of water and brought it back to Nugun. The Senar drank thirstily, wiped his mouth with the back of a hairy hand, and sat down on the grass.

"We stay here to find woman?"

"Yes. We stay here until she comes back. And you are going to tell me some things about your people and where they come from." Blade searched his mind, trying to pick out the best of the various questions there. He wanted the one that would get the most information out of Nugun and confuse him the least.

Finally Blade found what he wanted to say. "Nugun, who are the Hairless Ones?"

7

It took several exhausting hours with Nugun for Blade to get a picture of the world in the Mountains of Brega. Not that Nugun was either stupid or unwilling to talk—on the contrary, he had ample native intelligence. And he saw it as his duty to the new Hairless One who had spared his life to answer all the Hairless One's strange questions.

But Nugun knew only three hundred or so words to express all the concepts that his mind could conceive. And it was a long time before Blade knew even roughly what those words were. Much time was therefore wasted asking the Senar questions he could not even understand, let alone answer.

Even when Blade had figured out Nugun's limitations, matters still went slowly. Blade had to put each question into words in his own mind. Then he had to translate them into words that Nugun could understand. Finally he could ask the question—and settle back to wait for Nugun's answer. Again, Nugun was not slow or unwilling. But the new Hairless One was asking him about things he had never had to think about before in all the thirty-odd years of his life. Why should he think about them? They were part of the world, like the air he breathed and the water he drank.

But Nugun did his best, and his best soon became good enough. Blade was a fairly good rule-of-thumb anthropologist from his experience with the strange lands and stranger peoples of Dimension X. It took from noon until nightfall, but when darkness came

Blade had a rough notion of how the Senar and the Hairless Ones—the Blenar—lived in the Mountains of Brega.

The mountains themselves "went up to the sky," starting about three days' fast march from the western edge of the forest. That edge was about four additional days west of where Blade and Nugun were. From what Wyala had said, Blade knew that the forest also extended about the same four days to the east. It was another week beyond that across rolling plains to the city of Brega itself. Neither Wyala nor Nugun had any notion whether there might be other lands beyond Brega in any direction.

Nugun apparently knew nothing about the previous society in Brega or was unable to put what he knew into words. But from Wyala Blade knew that there had once been a normal society of men and women living more or less in harmony in the land of Brega. At least, so the legends went.

But this society had destroyed itself in a great and terrible disaster, a war brought on by the violence of the men. From Wyala's recounting of the legends of the war, Blade recognized atomic, chemical, and bacteriological warfare. How long ago the war had been, Blade had no idea. Certainly long enough for the land to recover and for the whole history of the war to become a hazy mass of legend.

The disaster had smashed the old society, but some of its people had survived. Most of the survivors were women, who decided that the violence of the men had been responsible for the war. Therefore they would build a society of women, with only enough men for breeding purposes. Enough of the knowledge of the old society survived to make this possible.

Unfortunately, there were inevitably surplus males. What to do with them? Regardless of their hatred and fear of male violence, the women could not uproot violence from themselves. So they decided to make the surplus males into game animals. They were released into the forests at the age of twelve or so. Then when they had reached the age of about twenty, hunting parties from the city slipped into the forests to track them down.

All of this Wyala had told Blade. The rest of the story he got from his talks with Nugun.

The women of the city did not catch all the men they released into the forest. Some at once fled farther west, toward the mountains, out of the reach of the hunting parties. Others learned so much skill in the woods that they could avoid the hunting parties. Sometimes they even turned the tables, making the huntresses the hunted. When they did that, they sometimes killed the women they caught outright. But at other times they enslaved them, perhaps later trading them to the mountain dwellers. In time, children began to be born of these strangely assorted matings.

Most of these children were Senar—the Hairy Ones. A few were of the Blenar—the Hairless Ones. No couple could tell in advance what their child might be. Whatever poison did this seemed to lurk in the air or the soil or the water, and there was no getting away from it. (Blade suspected it was a case of lingering radioactivity or bacterial contamination from the disaster.)

The time came when the women stopped releasing their surplus males into the forest to improve the game supply. There were enough of the Senar already.

"What about the Blenar?"

"Oh—Blenar not come into forest. Live in mountains. Not strong, I tell you. Women of city not know what are Blenar."

"I see."

So the women of Brega did not know that a race of intelligent males was growing up in those distant and inaccessible mountains. The years passed, and the number of men living in the mountains increased steadily. It was a harsh life, and many of the babies that were born did not live long. But there were many girls among those who did. In time it was no longer necessary to mate with women of the city captured in the forest. There were still not enough women to go around, however, and the Blenar usually wound up with more than their fair share. This would have meant war between the Senar and the Blenar, except that the Blenar's weapons were too good. Also, they taught the Senar many useful skills and made for them many things they could not have made for themselves. So there was an uneasy peace among the two kinds of men in the mountains.

More years passed, and the numbers of the men in the mountains increased still further. Blade could get only a very rough notion of how many there were now. Nugun could not count beyond a hundred. But Blade gathered that there were many more than a hundred clans and tribes among the Senar. And the area they occupied was nine days' march from north to south and three days' march from east to west. So there were a hundred thousand Senar, at least.

But in the last few years, some of the Blenar had been making friends with the Senar, or at least pretending to make friends. Nugun trusted no Hairless One's intentions toward his people, never had, and never would. Blade was no exception, for he was not really one of the Hairless Ones of the Mountains of Brega.

Many thousands of the Senar were listening to the Blenar, however. The Blenar were saying that the Senar could become the rulers of Brega. All they would have to do was learn the war skills that the Blenar could teach them and how to use the weapons the Blenar would give them. Then thousands of the Senar could march out of the mountains and through the forest and into the lands beyond the forest. They could take that land, where they could grow good crops and feed many children. Perhaps they could even take the city of Brega itself, with all its women. Then there would be a woman or even several women for every man old enough to know what to do with one, whether he was Blenar or Senar.

Blade could see how this might be a tempting vision

and how it had attracted many thousands of the Senar. But it had not appealed to Nugun.

"Nugun think Hairless Ones want to kill Senar so they have all land in mountains, all women. Blenar not strong to kill Senar themselves. So want women in city to do it. Blenar think good. But Nugun also think good, yes?"

"You do think good," said Blade. "Very good. I think that is exactly what the Blenar want to do with the Senar."

"Blade not want to do this with Senar? Not listen to other Hairless Ones?"

"The other Hairless Ones are bad people. I do not listen to bad people or help them do what they want to do."

"Blade think good, even more than other Hairless Ones," said Nugun with a broad grin.

Blade appreciated the compliment. But it did not take much "good thinking" to realize what a ridiculous project the Blenar had conceived. No number of Senar could hope to make headway against the bows and swords and throwing ropes of the fighting women of Brega. Perhaps in the forest they might have a chance. But the Blenar were apparently talking of a war down on the plains around the city. There the women would be on their home territory, fighting for their own way of life. And how many of the Senar could make the journey from the mountains, through the forest, and down to the plain? Ten thousand? That would be a generous estimate.

Blade sighed. Once more he seemed to have landed in a dimension where *none* of the people had anything worth taking back, or even worth fighting for. Blade could not help feeling that the wisest thing for him to do would be to give both Wyala and Nugun the slip. Then he could spend the rest of his time in this Godforsaken dimension prowling the forest, living on what he could catch and pick. Summer seemed to be coming on, and Blade knew more than enough about survival in the field.

But Wyala and Nugun had put themselves under his protection, and he could not abandon them. He would go with them to the Mountains of Brega. At least the mountain people would be less likely to shoot him on sight than the women of the city.

But Nugun was looking at Blade with a worried expression on his face. He appeared to be feeling for words to ask a question of his own.

"Blade not tell woman about Hairless Ones?"

"Why not?"

"Women not know about Hairless Ones. If they know, they maybe come into mountains. Kill all men, take women back to city. Hairless Ones make women in city afraid."

That made good sense to Blade. As long as the women of Brega thought they had only the violent but comparatively stupid Senar to deal with, they would continue to play their vicious little games with them in the forest. But if they realized that the men had now developed brains as well as brawn, a war of extermination might begin.

"I understand, Nugun. You are right. I will not tell Wyala." He doubted that he would ever even have the chance to break that promise. Wyala had been gone for nearly ten hours now. It seemed more than a little unlikely that she would ever be coming back.

But Blade still took the night guard duty. If Wyala did slip back in the hours of darkness, Blade wanted to be the one awake and on watch to greet her. Nugun had sworn to keep his hands off Blade's woman. But if Wyala returned to the camp while Blade was sound asleep, armed only with her knife—Blade didn't want to tempt Nugun that much right now.

Just as the eastern sky began to turn pale, he heard a soft voice calling from the trees on the far side of the stream.

"Blade? Are you there?"

"Is that you, Wyala?"

There was a small, indignant snort. "Of course it's me."

Blade nocked an arrow to the bow and trained it in the general direction of the voice. "Are you alone?"

"Yes."

"Then step out onto the bank of the stream." Blade almost trusted Wyala. But she might have fallen in with a hunting party from the city and changed her mind. Or the hunting party might be using her to bait a trap.

There was a rustling in the underbrush beyond the stream, and a familiar slim figure stepped out onto the bank. Blade examined her all over as carefully as the dim light permitted, without letting the arrow drop away from his bow. She looked more tired and dirty than before, but that was all.

Finally he nodded and called, "All right, you can come on over." She obeyed with a speed that suggested she was far from happy about standing there with her back to the dark forest. As she stepped up on the near bank of the stream, she saw Nugun's sleeping form sprawled on the ground beyond the campfire. She gave a little gasp.

"Is he dead?"

"No, only sleeping."

"Did you—beat him?"

"Yes. I defeated him in a fair fight, with my bare hands. The warriors of my people are taught to fight that way, as well as with weapons."

"But—is it—is he—?"

"He knows that you are my woman." Blade smiled reassuringly.

Wyala snorted indignantly. "No woman of the city can belong to a man. It is against the Laws of—"

"Perhaps," said Blade sharply. "But keep your voice down, you little fool! The Laws of Mother Kina have nothing to do with the way we are living now, here in the forest. Nugun cannot understand them, and I could not make him do so. As long as he thinks you are my woman, he will not touch you or harm you.

He has sworn to be my friend, to die for me if necessary, and to protect what is mine, even including my woman."

"But I tell you, I am not—"

"For your own safety, you had best keep your mouth shut about that. If Nugun comes to believe you are not really my woman—well, he will think he can do to you whatever he wants. Do you want to risk that, Wyala?"

Wyala gasped, then was silent. The silence continued.

"Well?" said Blade coolly.

Wyala swallowed. "I will be your woman, Blade."

"Good," said Blade. He went over to the sleeping Nugun and shook him by one thick-muscled shoulder. "Wake up, my friend. It is almost dawn, and my woman has returned. It is time to start on our march to the mountains."

They spent the first part of the day's march retracing the path Blade and Wyala had followed the morning before. They stopped about noon to refill their water bottles at a spring. Nugun dug under a bush with his bare hands, turning up half a dozen or so pale yellowish tubers about the size of small potatoes. He presented them to Blade with the air of one giving a valuable gift.

"Good to eat," he said. "Senar eat, in forests." Blade thanked the man and stowed the tubers away in his own sack. Then they moved on.

The afternoon's march took them into territory strange not only to Blade, but even to Wyala. Apparently the hunting parties from the city never went much farther west than their night's campsite, at least not any more. Once they had done so, but now the Senar in the western parts of the forests were too numerous. Some of the hunting parties that had gone far toward the mountains had never come back. Blade wondered if ambushes laid by the Blenar had something to do with this.

He also knew he would just as soon not find out

from personal experience. With a little luck and a lot of care he could easily protect Wyala from Nugun. But he doubted if he could do so against a dozen or a score of armed Senar, perhaps led by a Blenar. The farther west they got, the more careful they would have to be about hiding their tracks and camps and keeping a watch at night. He explained this to Nugun very carefully.

The Senar nodded. "I help you hide. Nugun know forest. Other Senar not get Blade's woman."

"Good," said Blade. Wyala merely sighed with relief. But she still did not take her hand far from the hilt of her knife.

Nugun did indeed know the forest and kept his promise better than Blade had dared hope. The Senar was brilliant at finding hard ground that would leave no tracks, leading them through streams to break their trails, and so forth. He even found a campsite for the night near another growth of the yellowish tubers. He dug up nearly two dozen more of them and showed Blade and Wyala how to split them and roast them on sticks over the fire. They were tasteless but filling.

After all three had eaten their fill, Nugun pointed to the ground. "Blade and woman sleep. Nugun watch tonight."

Blade was more than willing to lie down and drop off into a deep sleep. He had been marching or fighting or keeping watch for the better part of two days. But Wyala's eyes widened in fear. She stepped up close to Blade and whispered in his ear, "Can we trust him? Suppose he betrays us to all the other Senar? They would kill you and—"

Blade sighed wearily. "I do not think he will do that. I think he will be faithful to me."

"He is a man, Blade."

"I know that," said Blade shortly. He was becoming rather weary of Wyala's nervousness, although he could understand her reasons for it. "But a man can keep faith just as well as a woman. It's time you

72

started learning that. And even if he isn't trustworthy, it's better to find out now than when we're in the mountains. There aren't nearly so many Senar around here."

Wyala was still doubtful. Blade suspected that she would not sleep very well tonight. But he was not going to worry. Even if it turned out that Nugun could not really be trusted, there was nothing to do about it except kill him. He could not be watched every minute of the trip. Blade was damned if he was going to kill the Senar merely on Wyala's suspicions! He would trust Nugun unless and until the Senar betrayed that trust.

Nugun did not betray Blade's trust, not that night nor any day or night of the trip after that. He led them steadily westward, through country that was slowly but unmistakably rising. The forest was still as thick as ever, but the hardwoods now began to give way almost completely to evergreens. The undergrowth also began to get thinner, and patches of the yellow tubers were fewer and farther between. But Nugun was as reliable as ever in nosing out what was left. And there was plenty of small game for Blade's bow. They had to eat both tubers and meat raw, however. Nugun warned them that they were getting into country where it was not wise to build a fire if they did not want to be found. Blade and Nugun did not particularly enjoy the diet of raw food, but neither did they balk at it. Wyala, however, would not eat for a day, until hunger and weakness drove her to it.

Blade said nothing to Wyala about this, nor about her continued suspicion of Nugun. She was no fool, and he knew that she would make the right decision in her own time. But she was having more new experiences in a single week than she had had before in her whole life. It would take her a while to get used to things.

Nugun was certainly right about the Senar becoming thicker on the ground. Three times during the day

73

they had to hastily hide themselves to avoid roaming parties of them. None of them included any Blenar, however.

One night Nugun was mounting guard when a party of Senar approached. He promptly awoke Blade and Wyala and kept watch while they ducked under some bushes. Then hè scattered any signs of their camp before he joined them. After that night, Blade had no more doubts at all about Nugun's loyalty. Even Wyala stopped worrying about it.

Toward noon of the next day, the woods began to thin out noticeably. By midafternoon, the ground was rising more steeply than before. And just before they made camp for the night, Blade caught a clear glimpse of the western horizon. High above it, silhouetted against the blazing colors of the sunset, loomed the jagged masses of a mountain range. He looked at Nugun and pointed.

The Senar nodded. "Those are the mountains," he said.

8

Seeing the mountains looming up on the horizon did not at once make much difference to the three travelers. The settled areas on their lower slopes were three days farther on from where they were now. It might be longer if they had to spend time avoiding roving parties of hostile Senar. After a meal of raw squirrel's flesh, Blade took Nugun aside and asked him about this.

"You think good, Blade," said Nugun. "Yes. Senar not like to see you with your woman. They try to take, maybe kill if fight. Maybe kill you, me too."

"What about the Blenar?"

Nugun cocked his massive head to one side for a long time, considering the matter. "Many Hairless Ones want Senar to think Hairless Ones friends. They also take your woman, maybe use her, maybe give her to Senar. Not good Blenar for you, your woman."

Blade nodded. "Are there *any* Blenar I can trust not to hurt Wyala?"

Nugun was silent for an even longer time after that question. Blade began to wonder if perhaps he had asked a question about something that was taboo. Certainly Nugun looked like a man who knew the answer to a question but wasn't sure whether he should give it. He was wrinkling up his massive forehead into a frown and pulling at his thick lower lip with his fingers.

Finally he nodded. "Some Hairless Ones live in forest by Purple River. They say—Senar not go out with Hairless Ones to fight women, live in plains, take city.

Not good. Better live in mountains, learn to raise food here"—he waved his hand around them—"not fight women."

Blade wasn't sure what Nugun thought of this group of Blenar. So he only said, "That is a strange way of thinking."

"Not—strange," said Nugun sharply. "Think good. We go to city, women kill us all. Stay here, women come to us and we take easy. Here we know land, here we can fight them good. They know land by city, they fight good there."

"Exactly," said Blade, with a grin. He slapped Nugun hard on the shoulder. The Senar had stated perfectly the reasons for fighting on one's home territory. A trained professional soldier from Home Dimension could not have stated them as clearly and briefly. Then his grin faded. He would have to ask a ticklish question now.

"Nugun," he said quietly. "I think I am going to have to talk to Wyala about the Blenar around the Purple River. She must know about them."

Nugun did not show any anger. He merely looked puzzled. "Why, Blade?"

"From here on, we may be attacked by Senar or bad-thinking Hairless Ones at any time. Suppose I get killed. Then you will take her—"

"Nugun not take woman if Blade die. Nugun stay and die with him. Kill many bad Senar, Hairless Ones for Blade."

Blade shook his head. "No, Nugun. That is not the way I want it to be. If I am killed or hurt so that I cannot walk and run, you must take Wyala to the Purple River. Promise?"

After a moment, Nugun nodded slowly. "I promise."

"Good." Blade shook hands with the Senar. "But she might not go with you if she doesn't know where you are going. So I must tell her that you will be taking her to friends in the Purple River forest. Do you understand that?"

76

"Nugun not want woman to know about Blenar. Tell women in city. Women in city come—"

"The women in the city will *not* come," said Blade sharply. He was getting a little impatient with the stubborn man. "You have just told me that the women do not know this land, that they cannot fight good here. Didn't you?"

"Yes." The answer was reluctant and sullen.

"So there is nothing to be afraid of, even if the women do come. But they will not come, because my woman will not go back to the city. The Hairless Ones of the Purple River will keep her here in the mountains if I am killed. But you must take her to them if I die. You must promise to do that, if I am to believe that you will really follow me."

"Nugun follow Blade." And, after a pause, "Nugun take woman to Purple Forest."

Again Blade shook hands with the Senar and clapped him on the shoulder. Then he went back to Wyala and told her of his agreement with Nugun.

Wyala shuddered at the mere mention of the possibility of Blade's death. "I'd rather die. That Senar may be trustworthy as long as you're alive, but what if I'm alone with him?"

Blade sighed. "If you'd rather die, you'll have your knife and you can always use it," he said frankly. "But if you are willing to trust Nugun after my death, you have a chance of getting to the Purple River and living."

"Living in the mountains," she said pointedly.

"Of course," said Blade. He was also getting a little impatient with the woman. "Again, if you'd rather die . . ."

"No," she said hastily. "I will follow Nugun to the Purple River."

"Good," said Blade, with a sigh of relief. He kissed her. "You are a fine, brave woman, and make me think well of your city." That was almost telling the truth. "Now—let's get some sleep. Nugun will keep watch."

Nugun kept watch as faithfully as ever, and the

night was undisturbed. They scrounged some berries for breakfast and were on the move well before full daylight.

Moving across this open highland was different from moving through the forest. It would be almost impossible to meet any enemy unexpectedly. Nor could anyone readily lay an ambush for them. But there were also fewer places to hide. If they encountered an enemy, the odds were that they would have to fight.

They covered some twenty miles on their way to the mountains that day. The air was becoming noticeably thinner; Blade guessed they must already be more than a mile above sea level. Nowhere in all the highland they crossed did they find any water. By nightfall they had emptied their water bottles, but could find no place to refill them. Licking dry lips, Blade asked Nugun about the chances of finding water tomorrow.

"Oh—we find water tomorrow. No trouble," said Nugun cheerfully. "We go to Purple River forest, yes?"

"Of course."

"Then—big river on way. Much water. We have to swim river. But—" He hesitated.

"Yes?" said Blade.

"Many Senar live by river, catch fish. We cross river, they maybe see us, fight, kill."

"Maybe," said Blade. "But we will try to get there at night. They will not be able to see us so easily then."

"Good, good." Nugun nodded enthusiastically.

After a waterless and half-sleepless night, they pushed on. From what Nugun said, Blade guessed the river was just under twenty miles farther on. They pushed on hard for about ten, rested an hour, then pushed on for another five. Several times during this second stretch they saw moving parties in the distance. But none ever closed or showed any curiosity. Nugun was surprised at this, but after thinking it out had an answer.

"They see—we just three. Three people not kill, do

78

much. They not think about us." Blade hoped that Nugun was right and that the local Senar would go right on not thinking about his little party.

At the end of the five miles, Blade called a halt. The party went to earth in a nearby patch of shrubs like miniature fir trees. Blade's own throat felt as though it were filled with sand, and Wyala was on the point of collapse. But only five miles ahead lay water. Nugun didn't seem at all affected by the lack of water, any more than he had been affected by the lack of food or the hard marching or his injuries from the fight. The Senar seemed as tireless and tough as if he had been made of metal instead of flesh. Blade was gladder than ever that he had decided to try winning the man's loyalty and friendship, rather than just killing him. Without Nugun—and without Wyala—he would have a hard time getting anything worthwhile done in this dimension of more than usually strange peoples.

It seemed like forever before it happened, but eventually the sun went down and darkness covered the land. Flexing cramped and stiffened limbs, Blade rose to his feet and oriented himself. Straight ahead, on the route they had been following, lay the river. Without a word he urged his companions to their feet and led them out into the darkness.

Before they had gone more than a mile, the trees began to grow thick again. It soon became almost impossible to move as quickly and quietly as Blade would have liked. Blade was also worried about running into some night-prowling Senar by accident. "Senar sleep at night. Think night full of *dimbuli*—bad things," Nugun assured him. But the reassurance did not make Blade relax his alertness.

Another mile or so, and Blade saw the yellow glow of fires off to the right. But they were far away in the forest. He did not slow down. If they ran into anybody from that Senar village, it would be purely by chance.

The fire had just drifted out of sight behind them

79

when they came to a clearing. Blade led the way out into it, then froze abruptly. From behind a fallen tree he could see the faint glow of a small fire. In its light he saw four hunched shapes sitting around it. As Blade froze in mid-stride, one of them stood up, stretched, and turned toward him. A moment later, Blade saw light reflected off the man's eyes as he opened them wide, staring at the three figures coming out of the darkness. The man growled angrily and his comrades sprang to their feet, snatching up their clubs. In the next moment they were climbing over the log toward Blade, brandishing the clubs. Then Blade was running at the four, drawing his sword and knife with sharp metallic rasps as he ran. Nugun ran close behind him, waving his own club.

Nugun's mouth opened to shout a warcry. Blade looked back over his shoulder at the Senar and snapped, "Quiet!" The cry died. Then the four charging Senar were on them.

One rushed at Blade, swinging his club low. Blade danced out of the way, at the same time thrusting high with his sword. The point drove into the Senar's skull squarely between the eyes. Blade felt the thin bone shatter under the thrust. As he jerked his sword free, the Senar toppled and fell face down on the ground, to lie motionless.

The two Senar behind Blade's victim had to swing wide around the body of their comrade, which opened a gap between them. Blade leaped into it, clear over the body on the ground. In the same moment he thrust to the right with his sword and to the left with his knife. The knife drove into a meaty thigh and drew a howl of pain. But a club plunged down on his sword, smashing it out of his hand. It plunged point-down into the ground, and Blade frantically tried to fend off the Senar with his knife while shaking his numb and tingling right hand.

But the Senar did not follow up his victory. Clutching his club, he turned and plunged off into the darkness at a dead run, short legs churning frantically.

Blade let him go. Even if he had been able to use both hands, there was no sense in dashing off into the darkness, to blunder about in search of the fleeing Senar.

Instead he turned to help Nugun with his opponent. But as Blade turned, Nugun's club smashed down the other's clumsy guard and descended on his skull. There was a sound like a watermelon hitting a stone floor, and the last Senar also dropped. Like Blade's first victim, he did not even twitch.

Blade beckoned to Wyala, who had been hanging back out of the way while the two men fought. "We've got to move fast now," he said. "One of them got away, and he may give a warning." Wyala's face paled, but she nodded. Nugun merely growled defiantly and bent to wipe the blood off his club.

Blade led the others across the clearing at a run, slowing to a trot as they entered the forest on the other side. There were three miles to go to the river, more miles of populated territory on the other side, and not much time to cover both.

On they went through the dark forest, no longer daring to take the time to move slowly and silently. They plunged along, crashing through bushes, snapping twigs underfoot, occasionally tripping over outstretched roots. Blade went sprawling more than once, coming up with blood on his grazed cheeks and knees. Twice he had to help Wyala to her feet. Only Nugun never stumbled, but ploughed on, as noisy but nearly as unstoppable as a tank.

They must have covered nearly half the distance to the river before Blade saw the glow of any more fires. The first ones he saw were well off in the distance, so he did not bother even slowing down. A few minutes later, he saw a yellow glow coming closer, less than a hundred yards off to their right. He motioned the two behind him to slow down to a walk, and drew his sword. Step by step they slipped past the settlement, so close that Blade could see the bulky silhouettes of Senar against the fire. The moment he could be reasonably sure that the settlement was out of earshot, he sped up to a trot again.

They must have been less than a mile from the river when Blade heard sounds behind him. He whirled and stared back into the darkness, then at Nugun. The Senar had also heard something and was staring back, eyes wide. Finally he turned back to Blade with a grunt and said, "Men—Senar—come behind us."

Blade knew that the Senar's night vision was considerably keener than his own. "Following us?" he whispered.

"On same path. Not walk fast."

Perhaps they were not a search party, then. With luck and speed perhaps the three could outdistance those behind. Blade motioned Wyala to close in behind him. Then he broke into a run.

The three dashed through the woods even faster than before. Good luck and Nugun's eyes kept them from stumbling or going astray this time. But nothing could have kept them from making an uproar of footfalls, cracking branches, and heavy breathing. Before too long, Blade could look behind him and see the unmistakable lights of torches bobbing on the path, as the party behind them also increased its pace to a run.

Blade had no more doubt that the people behind them were after them. But there was nothing to do about it except keep running and hope to cross the river before the pursuers caught up with them. That would be easy for him and Nugun, but the pace was beginning to tell on Wyala. Sweat was streaming off her face now, and her mouth was wide open as she gasped for breath. Occasionally she lurched and reeled as she ran, but she never quite stumbled, never quite lost her footing.

Then the forest began to thin out around them, and in the darkness ahead Blade caught the faint glimmer of water. Within a few minutes, they were approaching the south bank of the river. At the same moment, Blade saw their pursuers burst out of the forest behind them. There were at least a dozen torches, and as they moved out into the open they spread out in a wide line, slowing down to a walk as they did so.

Blade turned back to the river, peering out into the darkness to pick out the far bank. He guessed it was a hundred yards away—a good healthy dip, to say the least.

Without a word Wyala bent and began removing her sandals, while Blade unstrung his bow and thrust the string inside his tunic. Hopefully that would keep it dry. Then he undid his own sandals and looked over his shoulder at the torches. They were still a good two hundred yards away, approaching cautiously. Did the people back there think that they had their prey trapped against the riverbank? They were going to get a surprise if they did. Blade turned and walked into the river.

The bottom dropped off swiftly, and in seconds he was swimming. The current was strong but not over-powering, and he was easily able to keep his head above water and push toward the opposite bank. The water itself felt refreshingly cool on his sweating body.

Behind Blade the others slipped into the river. Wyala gave a gasp as she entered the water and struggled for a moment. Then she gave a gasp of another sort as Nugun's massive right arm reached out to support her. She stared hard at him, eyes wide, then let him help her. Nugun ploughed through the water like a walrus, snorting and splashing so loudly that Blade had to tell him sharply to be more quiet. After that the Senar swam with steady, silent strokes that barely broke the surface.

They were halfway across the river before the line of torches reached the bank behind them. Looking back, Blade could see more than twenty men lined up along the bank, besides the dozen torch holders. One or two of the torch holders were waving their torches about like madmen. Now—if all those people would just stay where they were. Blade turned back and concentrated on his swimming.

Soon they were three-quarters of the way across. There was still no sign that the people behind them had figured out what had happened. Or perhaps they had, but none of them could swim, and they were going to have to waste time looking for a boat. The thought almost made Blade laugh out loud.

And now they were approaching the far bank. It was less than twenty yards away, heavily overgrown with bushes right down to the water's edge. Ten yards, and Blade felt weeds and thick mud underfoot. He let his feet drop down onto the bottom, but kept low and motioned the others to do the same. Still half-crouching, he covered the rest of the distance to the bank, then swiftly reached for a branch and hauled himself out of the water.

Splashes behind him told him that the other two were doing the same. Nugun was practically lifting Wyala out of the water. Then from within the bushes came the sound of running feet and crashing branches. Blade whirled so fast that he nearly slipped on the muddy bank, drawing his sword and shouting a warning in the same moment. Then the attackers burst out of the bushes with savage cries.

There were at least a dozen of them. For a moment Blade could only stare at the two men in the lead. Both were short, bearded, and stocky, but neither of them had much more hair than Blade himself, and their foreheads rose high above glaring black eyes. Both carried long, straight swords and large, round shields. They charged at Blade. Behind them came ten Senar, waving seven-foot spears. They plunged down the bank toward Nugun and Wyala.

As Blade met the rush of the two Blenar, he heard one of the Senar shout, "No kill woman! We want!" and the *wsssh* of thrown spears. Blade heard two of them splash into the water behind him.

He ducked under a whistling slash from the man on his right—fast but clumsy—and thrust under the edge of the shield at the man's knee. The sword point grated on bone, and the man screamed and staggered.

As he did, Blade grabbed him by his beard and pulled him around. He held the man in front of him as the other Blenar rushed in. The second man's sword slashed down as Blade thrust his prisoner forward. The prisoner let out another howl of agony as the descending sword sheared off his right arm. Blade released the man, then snatched the shield off the man's left arm and snapped it up in front of him. Now he had a shield as well as a sword and perhaps a chance, even against the other Blenar's longer sword.

But in that moment another scream tore into the air —a scream that could only have come from Wyala's throat. Blade spun around.

Wyala was kneeling on the bank, both hands clutching the shaft of a spear driven through her body just below the left breast. Blood was already trickling from the corner of her mouth and dripping down onto the muddy bank. Then she choked on the blood welling up in her throat and sagged forward. As she did, the butt of the spear caught in a root and the point broke through her back and stuck out behind her, red and dripping.

For one more moment the Senar stood paralyzed, staring at the dead woman. Then a tremendous uproar broke out, with curses, growls, and screams of rage and pain as they fought among themselves. Blade saw one Senar thrust with his spear into the groin of another—the one who had killed Wyala? Blade hoped so. The wounded Senar fell to the ground and rolled around, clutching at his wounds and howling in agony. Blade turned, looking for Nugun. If the Senar could attack that mob before it got itself sorted out—!

But Nugun was nowhere to be seen. No, there was a trace of him, and Blade felt a chill as he saw it. Out on the river, a few feet from the bank, was a spreading pool of blood. Even as Blade watched, the current caught it and it began to break up.

Blade cursed and turned back to the Blenar, with one grim determination in him—kill as many of the enemy as he could before they got him. He accepted

85

the fact that his luck had run out, but he still had some things to do before he would lie down and die.

He charged the Blenar and drove him back into the bushes until he could not retreat any farther. But the man was a good swordsman. With his shorter weapon, Blade could not close. He backed off, holding up his shield, backing to where the first Blenar lay, hoping for a moment to snatch up the fallen man's sword. His opponent followed him, but did not crowd close. The man had too much respect for Blade's strength and reflexes.

Two steps more—one step—there! The Senar were still fighting among themselves, and two more were down on the ground now. The first one lay still, unconscious or already dead from loss of blood. Blade began to allow himself a faint glimmer of hope. If he could kill his opponent before the Senar sorted themselves out, perhaps he might find a road to the Purple River. . . .

But as he bent to clutch the sword, there was more crashing in the bushes. Six more Senar and one of the Blenar burst out of the greenery, and these Senar were under control. Blade's opponent sprang aside from their path as they charged in. At a barked order from their own leader, all six reversed their spears, to come at Blade thrusting and swinging with the butts. Blade tried to back away, but he could not go far without running into the other group of Senar.

He fended off thrusts and swings with his shield and slashed away at the flailing spear butts with his sword. But his opponents still had the reach on him. His sword chopped through one spear shaft, then stuck in a second. The Senar's massive arm muscles twitched, the spear jerked up, and the sword snapped out of Blade's hands and flew into the air. Sickened, Blade watched it arc over the heads of the Senar and splash into the river. Then all six of his opponents came forward in a single rush, a solid wall of massive muscles and rank hair and foul breath.

Blade felt one spear swing low and scythe into the

side of his knee. He could not move to avoid the next spear, which thrust butt-first under his shield into his stomach. Agony tore through him and he tried to keep from doubling up, tried to keep his shield up. But one of the Senar got around to his left, and a spear came down on his shield arm with a crash. More agony. The shield sagged down, and as it did, two more spear-butts crashed onto Blade's exposed head. There was pain, there was flame and sparks before his eyes, and finally there was blackness.

9

Blade awoke slowly, conscious of pains everywhere he remembered being hit and a good many more in other places. He stretched his battered arms and legs one by one, wincing at the pain that shot through them. Life and circulation slowly returned to them. Then he opened his eyes and looked around him.

He was lying naked on a pile of straw on the dirt floor of a log hut. Chinks in the walls and roof let in enough light to indicate that it was daylight outside. Apart from the pile of straw, the hut contained only a small clay pot of water and a somewhat larger clay pot for wastes. Blade rose uncertainly to his feet, drank some water from the smaller pot, used the larger one, and tottered back to the straw. A number of large, black-shelled insects ran out of the straw as Blade sat down on it.

Gradually the fogginess left his head and the aches and pains left his body. He noticed that the door to the hut consisted of two large logs fastened cross-wise with smaller ones. It was not slung on any sort of hinges, but wedged from outside against the edges of the opening. Blade went over to it and gave it a few tentative pushes and kicks. It did not move at all. Getting out of here was not going to be a simple matter of breaking down the door. He went back to the straw pile and sat down again.

He felt in reasonably good physical shape now, except for being rather hungry. It had been a while since his last solid meal. But he could not help feeling rather depressed over the fates of Wyala and Nugun.

No doubt Wyala herself would rather have died than fall into the hands of the Senar. But she needn't have died at all if Blade hadn't been so determined to head west into the mountains in search of the Hairless Ones. The Hairless Ones! If the ones he had fought by the river were typical of the breed, they weren't much of an improvement over the Senar.

And Nugun was also dead, his body no doubt drifting away down the river. He needn't have died either, if Blade hadn't wanted him to follow and guide. The Senar had been faithful—and his reward had been a pointless death in the river. Blade was not feeling very proud of himself.

But there was even less point than usual to feeling sorry for himself. He had, after all, found the Blenar, which was why he had come into the Mountains of Brega in the first place. Admittedly, as a prisoner, his chances of learning about their ways, skills, and plans would not be good. But he had many years' experience of keeping his eyes and ears open under rough conditions and learning much from seeing and hearing little. And perhaps he need not stay a prisoner long.

Several more hours passed before anybody paid any attention to Blade. Then the thud of hammers sounded outside, followed by a number of voices. With a clatter and a bang the door fell outward. Two of the Senar spearmen came in and stood on either side of the opening, their spears pointed at Blade. Two Senar women then came in, the first that Blade had seen. They were only a little less massive than their mates, and almost as hairy. Blade could see that clearly, for the women wore only short skirts of filthy, stained cloth. Their odor in the badly ventilated hut made Blade wrinkle his nose.

The two women brought in a fresh pot of water and a large wooden bowl filled with broiled fish and raw vegetables. Then they backed out, the spearmen followed, and the door was hammered back into place.

Except for being practically unsalted, there was

nothing wrong with the food. And Blade was hungry enough to have eaten things far less appetizing than the fish and vegetables. He emptied the bowl in a few minutes, drank some water, and settled back to wait for his captors to make their next move. The meal resolved one point—someone was determined to keep him alive, at least for the time being. For what?

Blade got no answer that day, nor the next, nor the day after that. He was fed twice a day, morning and evening, always the same broiled fish and raw vegetables. They began to get a little monotonous by the third day. The Senar women also gave him plenty of water and a fresh waste pot every morning. On the third day they even gave him a pile of clean straw. But neither the spearmen nor the women nor the ones who opened and closed the door ever spoke to him. They looked at him with open curiosity, but said not a word.

By the fourth day, Blade was beginning to wonder what the plans were for him—assuming that anybody here had any. If nobody did, he might not die of thirst, hunger, or mistreatment—but he might come close to dying of boredom.

The morning of the fifth day came, and with it the usual gaggle of Senar bringing the morning fish and vegetables. This time, however, four Blenar were with them, armed with shields, swords, and short-handled axes, and wearing heavy leather helmets with cheekpieces.

Their leader stepped forward, drew his sword, and said in a loud, hectoring voice, "Come with us. Rilgon would see you."

"Oh." Blade crossed his arms on his chest. "Indeed." His tone was very cool. He wanted to start off his relations with the local Blenar by refusing to be pushed around. "Who is Rilgon and why would he see me?"

The Blenar leader took a backward step, his face working in surprise. Apparently he was used to having prisoners cringe submissively before his drawn sword

Come for the filter...

A PRODUCT OF *Lorillard*

KENT

WITH

THE FAMOUS MICRONITE FILTER

DELUXE LENGTH

...you'll stay for the taste.

DELUXE LENGTH

WITH
THE FAMOUS MICRONITE FILTER

KENT

A lot of good taste
that comes easy
through the
Micronite filter.

18 mg. "tar," 1.2 mg.
nicotine av. per cigarette,
FTC Report Oct. '74.

Warning: The Surgeon General Has Determined
That Cigarette Smoking Is Dangerous to Your Health.

and loud, arrogant manner. There was a long silence, during which Blade continued to stare at the Blenar. He stared so effectively that the other three began to fidget nervously. Finally the leader, lowering his voice, said, "Rilgon is the War Leader of the Blenar. He has come from a great distance to see you, because he has heard that you are a warrior beyond anything dreamed of before in Brega. He would ask you to march with us against the city."

"Very well," said Blade. "Now that you have answered my questions, I will come with you. But I must have some clothes first. A warrior of my people does not appear before his future leader naked."

Both the request and the remark about "future leader" seemed to further confuse the Blenar. There was a long pause before the leader barked an order. One of the other Blenar scuttled out and returned a few minutes later with a tunic and sandals. Blade considered asking for weapons, but decided not to push his luck too far. He had already gained as much of a psychological edge as he was likely to get.

The four Blenar formed a square around Blade and marched him out of the hut. Outside, he found himself in the muddy main street of a Senar village of log huts. In front of each hut was a rough hearth of soot-blackened stones. Senar women were tending cooking pots bubbling on these hearths, while Senar men tramped up and down the "street" bearing massive loads of fish and wood. Senar children, stark naked and even filthier than their parents, ran in and out of the huts. Some of them stopped to stare at Blade and his escort tramping through the village.

The path sloped down, and Blade could see the waters of the river gleaming through the trees ahead. Just beyond the last hut was a small clearing on the edge of the trees. Blade looked at it casually—and stopped abruptly as he saw what was there.

A large square frame of logs had been erected in the middle of the clearing. A nude woman was spread-eagled on that frame, wrists and ankles tied to the logs with heavy vines. Even at a distance Blade could see that the woman's hands and feet had already turned white and bloodless from the tight knots. He looked more carefully and realized that the woman was tall and slender, and that her filthy hair and skin had both once been fair.

"A woman of the city?" Blade asked the leader.

"Indeed," said Blenar. "She was taken all of two years ago, so she should have learned the ways of the mountains by now. But she rebelled against her Senar master. The ways of the mountains shall prevail."

"What will happen to her?"

"She has been tied up there for two days and nights already, without food or water. Tomorrow night she will receive two hundred lashes. If she survives that, she will be turned out into the forest, to live or die as the will of the mountains may have it."

"Probably die," Blade was keeping his voice tightly under control. Also his stomach.

"Yes. Most of them do. But what would you have us do with rebels?"

"I will make no suggestions, friend. The ways of your people are not the ways of mine." That was a polite statement that could hardly get him in trouble for the moment. Matters might well be different when he faced Rilgon.

Rilgon was living in considerable state aboard the barge in which he had come down the river to meet Blade. It was a large, slab-sided craft with no pretense at grace or sea-worthiness. It was moved by twelve long sweeps pulled by Senar oarsmen and a single large square sail. A number of armed Blenar were lounging on the grimy deck when Blade's escort marched him up to the foot of the gangplank. They promptly took charge of Blade and led him aboard the barge.

Rilgon met Blade in the cabin on the stern of the barge. It was a low-windowed, low-ceilinged affair, dark and obviously none too clean. Rilgon himself was lying on a pile of roughly sewn cushions. A long pipe drooped from his thick, bearded lips and a jeweled

92

sword lay on the floor within easy reach of one thick-fingered hand. In fact, everything about the man was thick and gross. He was almost as physically massive as a Senar, and with only a little more hair on his heavy belly he could have passed for one.

Blade carefully kept any expression of distaste off his face and gave Rilgon his standard story about being a traveling warrior from a far-distant land. The story had served him well among a variety of people in a variety of dimensions, and Blade saw no need to change it here. It explained his undeniable skills as a fighter, but did not promise too much. This was particularly important here and now. The last thing Blade wanted to do was to make any definite promises to Rilgon.

Rilgon seemed to find the story acceptable. "Well, Blade," he said. "So you are a warrior."

"That is what I said."

"In fact, you are a warrior of quite marvelous skill. The tales of the fight by the river are traveling all over the mountains. When they came to my ears, I knew that I had to come and see you for myself."

"I am honored," said Blade. He managed to say that with a straight face.

"You should be," said Rilgon tonelessly. "I am Rilgon, War Leader of the mountains. Before three more moons have passed, I will rule in all of Brega, even in the city where now the evil women worship Mother Kina. Those who do not honor me will not live."

Blade suppressed a weary sigh. Megalomaniacs were, to say the least, rather tedious. "I can and will live to serve the new master of Brega, if indeed he becomes such. I have heard of the plans of yourself and the Blenar who follow you, and I find them very bold."

Rilgon's eyes narrowed and his hand moved toward the hilt of the sword. Blade tensed, for a moment fearing that he had gone too far. "Too bold?" the War Leader said in a chill voice.

"I cannot say that, Rilgon. I do not know all that

93

concerns your war against the women of the city. So I cannot speak surely of your war. But I am a warrior of many years' experience elsewhere, and I have seen many wars. By what I have seen in them, I find the war that is talked of very bold, and I would be speaking falsely to you if I said otherwise. You would not wish me to speak falsely, would you?"

"I would not. But never fear. It is known to me that the women of Brega will prove fatally weak when my warriors strike. I am not at all too bold, Blade. I am wise, for I know that the best moment to strike is when the enemy is at his weakest."

Blade nodded. "Indeed that is wise for a warrior." Rilgon's tone had made it clear that questions about the nature of the city's weaknesses would not be welcome.

Rilgon inclined his head and smiled with a graciousness so nauseating that Blade would have cheerfully strangled the man on the spot if he could have gotten away with it. But he knew that was not in the cards. What he would do, however, was set about making his escape as soon as possible. That decision made, he concentrated on keeping any sign of it off his face.

Rilgon continued, "I understand your woman was killed in the battle by the river when my warriors took you."

"Indeed she was," said Blade. "And I am much grieved and angered by it." For once he could speak his true emotions.

"I understand that you might be," said Rilgon, with another imperially gracious smile. "Be assured that those of her killers who were not slain by each other's hand on the riverbank will be found and punished."

"I am grateful." Blade decided that it was his turn to bow his head.

"It is the least I can do for one I hope to see at my right hand when I rule in Brega," said Rilgon. "But I shall do more. When I rule in Brega and all its women are mine, you shall have the choice of not one but three of the fairest. They shall serve all your wants and be subject entirely to your discipline."

"Even to the frame and the whip?" asked Blade.

"Even so," said Rilgon. There was an unmistakable look of anticipation on his dark, sweating face at the mention of punishment. "You have seen the girl tied out in this village, I suppose?"

"I have."

"You are luckier than I, for you will be here tomorrow night to witness her punishment. I, alas, must return north this very night, to continue my work, that the mountains may rule over the city."

"You assume great burdens for us all," said Blade. If he had to throw one more gross piece of flattery at this fat megalomaniac, he suspected he was also going to throw up his breakfast.

But Rilgon merely nodded in response, as though recognizing an obvious and undeniable truth. Then he raised his hand and said, "You may go."

Blade had been half hoping for some words about being set free. But none came, and he knew enough not to ask about the matter if Rilgon did not raise it himself. There would be time enough to make his escape, now that he had decided it was necessary.

So he merely bowed as low as he could comfortably manage and backed out. The Blenar of the barge crew escorted him down the gangplank and turned him back into the hands of the four who had brought him from the hut. Those same four then marched him back the way he had come.

As they marched past the clearing where the girl was tied, Blade noticed that she had raised her head. Wide brown eyes stared into his through a screen of small, whining insects. He could see a tongue already swollen from thirst protruding through cracked lips. But she did not speak, did not even moan. She merely looked at him, as though trying to decide whether or not he was real. Blade would have liked to stop and say something to her, but he doubted if that would be appreciated by his escort. And what could he say to her, in any case? He could hardly promise her any help.

The four Blenar led Blade up the main street of the village again and back to the hut. They wedged the door shut again, and the rest of the day passed as the four preceding ones had done. Eventually darkness came down on the village, and the only light coming through the chinks in the logs was from the fading cook-fires. There was nothing else to do, so Blade lay back on his pile of straw and went to sleep.

10

Blade awoke suddenly, with a noise in his ears that sounded like people screaming. As the sleep-fog cleared from his head, he realized that he was hearing exactly that. He could also hear from outside the hut people running and the clash of weapons. Frantically moving lights glimmered through the chinks in the logs.

Blade sprang to his feet, wishing that there was something in the hut he could use as a weapon, even a loose floorboard. But he could only stand there, fists clenched in impotent frustration, waiting for whatever was happening outside to sort itself out.

That did not take long. He had been awake and alert for barely a minute when hammers sounded outside. They were working on the braces of the door, and Blade could see it shaking. He flattened himself against the wall to the left of the door opening. Perhaps he could jump whoever was going to be charging through the door in a moment, get their weapons—

"Blade!" came a shout from outside. Blade was silent. The shout came again. Then the voice went on angrily, "Blade, are you there? We are from the Purple River, come to rescue you. Nugun reached us!"

Blade started. In the next second the door toppled with a crash. Two Blenar leaped over it into the hut. They whirled as they saw Blade crouched against the wall.

"You're safe, thank the Spirit of Union. Nugun was afraid—"

"Nugun? He reached the Purple River?"

"Of course. Would we be here if he hadn't?" snapped one of the men. "Now for the Spirit's sake and your own life, come on with us and stop talking! We've come with thirty men into a land where Rilgon can call out a thousand! Come on!"

Blade moved. The two Blenar might not be telling the whole truth, but at least they seemed willing enough to get him out of Rilgon's hands. For the moment he would be content with that.

As the three men burst out of the hut, two of Rilgon's Blenar warriors came dashing up, swords drawn. There was a brief and deadly flurry of clanging weapons. One of the Blenar ran off screaming, left wrist a bloody stump. The other folded in the middle and toppled, to lie face down beside the bodies of two dead Senar. Blade bent down to snatch up the dead man's weapons.

As he did so, a furious yelling and screaming burst out to his right. Blade looked that way and saw a mass of Senar storming forward, with a dozen Purple River Blenar slowly giving way before them. The Senar struck desperately with their clubs and thrust with their spears, but even when the blows went home, the Blenar did not go down. Blade realized that the Purple River men were wearing heavily padded, boiled-leather jackets and thighpieces, which could easily turn aside a Senar spear point.

One of Blade's rescuers jerked his arm. "Come on. We'll have to cut down along by the river and head north." Blade nodded; then a thought struck him.

"We can save the girl, then."

"What girl?"

"There's a city girl tied up for punishment down at the river end of the village. She'll be flogged to death tomorrow."

"Oh, damn!" said one of the Blenar. "We can't take the time, Blade. She—"

"She'll die tomorrow if we don't rescue her. I've already gotten one woman killed since I came to Brega. I'll be damned if I let another die when I could save her." He headed down the path at a trot. After a moment the two Blenar shrugged wearily and followed him.

The three men ran down the path to the clearing. Behind them the sounds of battle suggested that the Blenar were slowly retreating before the attacks of the villagers. As they passed huts, Blade noticed Blenar standing outside some of them, swords drawn; Senar—some of them women—lay dead or dying on the trampled and blood-spattered grass. As the three men passed, the Blenar on guard fell in behind them, one by one.

They reached the clearing just as a dozen of Rilgon's warriors burst into it from the opposite side. One of them ran straight at the bound girl, sword raised to run her through and put her forever beyond rescue.

Blade bent, one arm dipping to snatch up the spear of a fallen Senar. Then the arm straightened with a snap, and the spear flashed across the clearing and into the warrior's back. He threw his arms up, sword flying into the air, and toppled. Blade followed the spear across the clearing, cut down another warrior who ran at him, and reached the girl. Quick slashes with his own sword, and the ropes fell away.

As they did, the girl collapsed to the ground, eyes rolling up in her head. For a moment Blade thought she was dead; then he saw a faint motion of her breast. Thrusting his sword into his belt and dropping his shield, he got the helpless girl up on his back.

When he raised his head, he saw that Rilgon's warriors had either fled or gone down. Most of those who had gone down lay still on the tramped-down earth of the path, but some were still writhing and moaning. Blade and two of the Purple River Blenar moved among them, putting them out of their pain.

They had just finished doing this when the Purple River rear guard came up. Behind them Blade could see a much reduced group of Senar, several of them wounded, all of them hanging back at a safe distance. Without a word, the Blenar leader pointed at the woods along the river. The rescue force formed a double line and turned off the path.

They moved north along the bank of the river for nearly two hours, not stopping or slowing below a fast jog. For all his iron endurance, Blade found himself hard put to match the pace with the extra burden of the girl on his back.

The two hours passed without incident, however. Perhaps they had outrun warning of their presence. Or perhaps the local Senar took one look at the force of grim-faced, armored Blenar pounding along the riverbank and thought better of tackling them. There were twenty-four left out of the thirty that had come into the village. Behind them lay nearly forty of Rilgon's men, both Blenar and Senar.

After about two hours the raiders paused for a short breather in a particularly dense and deserted patch of forest. Blade sat down with a thud and let the girl slide to the ground. She was still unconscious, but breathing regularly, and circulation was obviously returning to her hands and feet. By morning she might be able to walk.

Blade would have liked to ask a few questions about who his rescuers were, where they were taking him, and why. But before he could get up enough breath to say a word, the leader called everybody to his feet. Two of the warriors picked up the girl between them, to relieve Blade. Then the whole party set out again, this time veering sharply to the northwest, away from the river.

They marched, with only one more stop, until well after dawn. By then they were deep into the forest, and there had been no sign of pursuit since they left the first village. But the leader was still careful to hide the camp in thick undergrowth and brush away his raiders' tracks for many yards back. Only then did he unsling his own shield and weapons and pull off his helmet.

Blade was prepared to respect the leader for this. However, that did not mean he was willing to keep from asking any of the pointed questions he had in mind. Blade got the girl awake and gave her some water. Her name was Melyna, and she had been taken prisoner in the ambush of a hunting party. She had tried to adapt to Senar captivity as best she could, horrifying as it was, in the hope of somehow being able to escape. But there had been no chance. Finally she simply didn't care any more whether she lived or died. Hence the rebellion and the death sentence from which Blade had rescued her.

When he had finished listening to Melyna, Blade rose and went over to where the leader was sitting on the grass, rubbing his sword with oil from a small copper vial. He looked up as Blade approached.

"Greetings, Blade. You have come to satisfy your curiosity on various matters, have you not?"

Blade nodded emphatically. "Such as who you are, where you are from, where you are taking me, and why."

The leader chuckled. "Indeed the first is easy. My name is Himgar. I am War Councilor to the people living in the forests around the Purple River. I am in fact to my people what Rilgon is to his. Who and what are you?"

Blade gave his usual story. Himgar listened, nodding with interest at various points. "We had gathered from what Nugun told us that you were a mighty warrior from a distant land. He—"

"How is he?"

"Nugun? He was wounded in the shoulder in the attack by the river and fell into the water. He wanted to rejoin you and die beside you. But then he realized that you might be captured, and he should go to the Purple River and tell the people there about you. In spite of his wound, he made the journey.

"He is not only unusually intelligent for one of the

101

Senar, but incredibly loyal. The fact that you had won such loyalty from one of the Senar was one of the things that decided us to send a rescue party. After that, it was simply a matter of marching and fighting. As you can see, none of Rilgon's fighters, Senar or Blenar, can stand against us." The last was not said boastfully, merely as a fact of life.

Blade nodded. "Then why have you not moved against Rilgon and destroyed him?"

Himgar shook his head wearily. "All of the Councilors would give up their souls to the Spirit of Union gladly if we could do that. But we are less than five thousand all together, and barely one out of four of these is a trained and armored warrior. Rilgon could mass ten times that many within a few days, and they would drag us down the way wolves drag down a stag. The Purple River would be defenseless, our lands would be overrun, and the last hope of Brega would perish with us."

"How are you the last hope of Brega?" Blade neither could nor would keep a slight note of skepticism out of his voice. He did not want to seem too willing to join anybody, even someone as apparently brave and honest as Himgar.

"We who worship the Spirit of Union dream of a world where men and women live together in peace, neither despising and abusing the other, both working to build and not to destroy."

"A dream indeed," said Blade. "You wish to rebuild your land as it was before the disaster."

Himgar shot him a sharp look. "You are familiar with our history, then—or at least our legends?"

Blade nodded and explained how he had talked with Wyala and Nugun.

"You seem to understand the dream, then," said Himgar. "Is it perhaps because in your homeland men and women live like that?"

"To some degree, yes," said Blade.

"Then perhaps you will understand why Rilgon must be defeated?"

"No, I do not." Blade actually suspected he did, but he wasn't going to give Himgar an easy victory by admitting that right away.

"Rilgon seeks to march on the city of Brega with his followers, thousands of Blenar and tens of thousands of Senar. He would destroy the city and all its works, take all its land, enslave all its women, and divide them among his followers."

"I know," said Blade. "He also thought I was worth a visit. He came down the river on his barge to see me and offered me many women and much power if I would serve him."

Himgar's nerves were not quite proof against that bold announcement. He swallowed. "You talked with —him?"

"Yes. And I pretended to accept his offer. I wasn't going to give him an excuse to kill me on the spot. Do you take me for a fool, Himgar?" Blade put more anger in his voice than he really felt.

"No, Blade," said Himgar. "I do not. But I hope you can at least see why Rilgon must be stopped."

"I can see *why*, Himgar. But I do not see that I need to take much of a hand in doing it. If he tries to march that rabble of his down to the city, the women will simply have better hunting without having to go into the forests to get it."

Himgar sighed. "I wish by all that I believe that this were true. But Rilgon's army will not fall on a united city."

Blade's eyebrows went up. So there was something to Rilgon's talk about a fatal weakness among the city's women. "Explain, please."

As quickly as possible, Himgar did so. There was a struggle going on in the city to choose the new Mistress of Fertility, who had charge of the House of Fertility and everything in it. Obviously, it was a vitally important post, and the two factions struggling for it spent all their time watching each other and none watching the forest that bordered the male-ruled lands. Even the routine patrols of the farmlands around

: city had been abandoned. A few hunting parties
ll went out, but that was all. Even within the city
self, the fighting women of one faction would not
submit to the orders of commanders from the other.

"So Rilgon's army will march across the lands of
the city and up to its walls with small danger of being
seen. It will fall on a city unwarned, unprepared, and
divided almost beyond defending itself. And the city
will fall, and much of our hope for Brega with it."

"How is that?" said Blade. "I did not think you
had so much love for the women of the city and their
ways. I certainly do not."

"I know," said Himgar wearily. "But I ask you to
believe me. Even in the Purple River lands, we have
almost none of the knowledge from before the disaster.
And Rilgon's people have even less.

"But in Brega they have much of it, at least in
medicine and other arts of that kind. We have some
hundreds of sympathizers in the city, who have been
passing that knowledge on to us bit by bit. It has been
slow, but we have been making things better for ourselves here by the Purple River. All of those who have
worked for us, risked their lives for us, will die if the
city falls.

"And even if there were no such women in the city,
we still would not want it to fall. For the knowledge
of old arts is still there as long as the city stands. If
the city dies, so does the knowledge. And it will stay
dead for the Spirit knows how many thousands of
years, until time brings it back to our descendants, or
men and women alike perish and leave the land to
the animals and the insects."

Himgar's voice had risen to a passionate crescendo
as he made his prophecies. Blade could not doubt the
man's sincerity. But Himgar didn't seem to have any
specific plan to prevent the disaster. Blade did not
think much of causes without plans.

"What are you planning to do?" he asked bluntly.

Himgar was ready with an answer. "We are going
to lead the people of the Purple River lands down to

the city. The women who have worked for us there will come out to join us. Then we shall all march north, over the mountains where they come down to the ocean. We have sent explorers into the lands there, and they are good lands. We and the women will go there and a new people will take root and grow."

"I see." Blade was telling the truth when he said that. He was not sure that he *believed* in Himgar's dreams, though. At best, it was a desperate solution— but perhaps Himgar saw the problem as desperate too. It was not really his place to judge. Certainly working for Himgar would be better than serving Rilgon. Meanwhile—

"What exactly do you want me to do?"

"We must send a small party of scouts to the city, to warn the women to be ready to march out and join us. That party will be better off if they can fight without arms as well as with them. Nugun said that you are marvelously skilled in fighting only with your hands and feet. Can you teach the other scouts to do the same?"

Blade hesitated. He was not going to promise miracles, even to keep Himgar happy. But he probably wouldn't need to perform any. If unarmed combat was a comparatively unknown skill in Brega, even a few weeks' training should be of great benefit to the scouts. It would certainly be enough to give any of the women of the city a nasty surprise.

"How much time will I have?" Blade asked.

"Not more than one moon-span. By the time the next moon-span is half gone, the scouts must be on the march for the city."

Blade considered this. About a month to train the scouts. About six weeks before they marched out.

"I shall give you my best," he said.

Himgar could not keep back a sigh of relief.

11

Two days' hard marching, and the raiders with Blade and Melyna reached the Purple River settlements. Melyna kept on her feet with the rest during those two days; her white, sweating face told of the courage it cost her. Once more Blade had to acknowledge the courage and determination of the women of the city. Disunited they might be, but Rilgon was going to have a fight on his hands that might well bleed his own people white. Blade hoped so.

On the morning of the third day they reached the main settlement. Looking down into the river through the tall ferns along its bank, Blade could see how it had gotten its name, for as far as the eye could see, the river bottom was a mass of dark purple gravel, tinting the clear water running over it.

Blade's contemplation of the river was broken by a sudden, explosive roar that could not have come from any normal human throat. He spun around, snatching his sword clear. Then he dropped the sword and held up his arms as he saw Nugun come dashing out of a hut toward him.

The Senar's right shoulder was heavily bandaged. But his rush nearly sent Blade flying back into the river, and his embrace nearly cracked Blade's ribs. He jumped up and down several times before he could finally speak.

"Blade here, Blade here, Blade here," he kept saying. The Senar was nearly incoherent with happiness. Blade himself could not help grinning broadly. He

106

gave the hairy man a clap on the shoulder that would have flattened a normal human.

"Thank you, Nugun," said Blade, when the Senar had calmed down. "I owe you a lot for that trip. And Melyna owes you her life."

Nugun's eyes took in the girl, and his face fell. "Nugun sorry Blade not have Wyala now. Nugun sorry not save Blade's woman."

Blade shrugged. "Yes, it is sad. But she was dead before you could have done anything to save her. Do not feel badly about it. You will have plenty of chances to avenge her."

"Yes." Nugun's head bobbed enthusiastically. "Nugun kill many Hairless Ones, bad Senar, send them after Wyala." He took another look at Melyna. "Blade have new woman now?"

Blade also looked at the girl. Melyna was looking about her curiously, although she was obviously almost ready to pass out on her feet from exhaustion. But the sight of civilized men and civilized women living and working together was too strange for her.

Blade shook his head. "She is not my woman, at least not now. And I do not think right now she even wants a man. She was a prisoner of the bad Senar for two years."

Blade was wrong about Melyna, as he discovered later that night. Himgar led him to a hut in the heart of the settlement and told him to relax and wait.

"For what?" said Blade. He looked dubiously around him at the hut. It was cleaner than the one where he had been a prisoner. It also had a bed, table, chairs, a small charcoal brazier, and other luxuries. But Blade wondered if he hadn't exchanged one captivity for another.

The War Councilor looked genuinely horror-stricken when Blade mentioned the possibility and shook his head sharply. "No, no, not at all, Blade. It is just that—well, I am only one of several Councilors to our people. And they must all agree to my plan for you before you can go to work. Until that time you would be wise to stay here, within this hut. Our people have small love for strangers. Were you to wander about at night, the Spirit alone knows what might happen to you. And believe me, I do indeed want your aid in the saving of our people."

Blade could not doubt the man's sincerity. But he was no more willing than before to be tamed. "Very well," he said coolly. "I shall wait while you try to convince the other Councilors that I can be trusted. But if you cannot, do not expect me to sit around in this hut forever. I will go out into the forest and live there, and be damned to you and Rilgon and the city and everybody else in Brega!" The flare of anger in that last sentence was genuine; Blade did not like this kind of game-playing.

Himgar left him, and the hours passed on toward night. A meal was brought—a thick stew of game and the yellow tubers in a wooden bowl, and sour, purplish wine in a wooden cup. Blade emptied both cup and bowl with a ready appetite, then lay down on the bed. It was not much cleaner than the pile of straw back among Rilgon's people had been, but it was a good deal warmer and more comfortable. He pulled the blankets over him and drifted off to sleep.

Tired as he was, Blade let himself sleep so deeply that nothing short of an earthquake could have wakened him. He did not wake until morning. When he did, he noticed two things. A pale pink light was already creeping in through the chinks in the logs. And there was something warm and soft and gently breathing snuggled up against him in the bed. Very slowly he turned to look at that "something," one hand creeping toward the knife under his pillow.

He was not surprised to see Melyna. She had managed to wash some of the filth of Senar captivity from her skin and hair. The hair now gleamed pale gold in the dawn, spread out on the pillow.

As though Blade's eyes on her had been a caress, Melyna stirred. Blindly she turned her head toward Blade, then opened her eyes. They were dark blue, and stared up at Blade without fear or even timidity. And why should she be fearful or timid? She had undoubtedly seen and even done things that would turn Blade's stomach in the past two years. Slowly, as though he were reaching out for a shy kitten he didn't want to frighten away, Blade laid a heavily muscled hand on one bare, tanned shoulder.

It was like ice melting. Melyna seemed to flow up and over on top of Blade. He felt a long, slim body pressing hard against him. He felt his own responding to the warmth and the pressure and the movement. He threw off the blankets, and his arms went around Melyna. She stiffened for a moment, then became even warmer and pressed even harder against Blade.

Melyna was really not soft at all. Under the tanned skin there were muscles toughened into whipcord by two years' back-breaking labor for the Senar. Her breasts and hips and buttocks were firm and solid, but spare of flesh, barely breaking the outline of her bones. It was almost like making love to the sketch of a woman.

But it was a warm, living, breathing sketch. And it was breathing harder and harder, as it wriggled and writhed and heaved under the movement of Blade's hands. He was being as gentle as if Melyna had been made of sand that would crumble away under too rough a touch. Before long, it was clear that he didn't need that kind of gentleness. Melyna was too ecstatic over making love to a civilized man after two years of barbarians to care very much.

So Blade's hands roamed all up and down Melyna's body, and hers did the same on his. He felt his own erection tightening into a solid, burning rod as small hands stroked and caressed, small, hard nipples traced patterns on his chest. She wriggled up on him even farther, and his lips brushed across her throat and over the bones that stood out in her thin neck. He kept on kissing her, down across the shoulder blades, down under one breast and up onto its long, jutting brown nipple, across to the other nipple, then back and forth

109

between them for a long time. By the time Blade's lips moved away from her breasts, Melyna was whimpering and sobbing deep in her throat, and her breath was coming with a rasp.

Again Melyna shifted up—and this time as she settled down, she placed herself squarely on Blade's upthrust phallus. She stiffened for a moment as the solid rod of flesh drove upward. Her mouth opened in a tremendous gasp. Then Blade pushed his own hips up, Melyna pushed hers down, and his solid, swollen member drove all the way into an already slick-wet canal.

For a moment after that Melyna did not move. Then she began to rock slowly back and forth, occasionally shifting from side to side. She was not tight, but her movements kept a continuous friction on Blade and a continuous arousal in him. He found his own hips beginning to move up and down. Occasionally his upward thrusts would meet Melyna coming down, and her eyes would widen as she felt him driving deep within her. Other times he would sink down as Melyna rose up. Then her face would contort with a feeling of loss, and she would promptly sink back down, trying desperately to recapture what seemed to be slipping out of her.

This went on long enough for Blade to lose all track of time, and for a good long while after that. Melyna's movements became faster and faster, until she was practically swinging herself around in a circle centered on Blade's maleness. Her hips gyrated wildly —and then all her pelvic muscles began jerking convulsively. Her head went back, her eyes closed, her face contorted from the delicious agony pulsing through her, while she gulped for air like a dying fish. Below, Blade felt a hot, warm gushing all over his groin and the frantic contractions of the canal embracing him.

Blade held on for a little while longer, although it seemed like a very long while indeed. But eventually he could no longer do anything except thrust frantically upward to make a desperate final few strokes.

110

Then he felt the beginning of his release, the frantic, furious pumping, and after another incredibly long time, the final fading away. He sagged back on the bed, every part of his body going limp and for the moment useless.

After a little while the fog cleared from Blade's head and the limpness left his muscles. He sat up, patted Melyna on her flat, hard stomach, and rolled himself out of bed to start the day. There was a large jug of water on the table by the bed, and Blade spent a long time splashing it on his face and chest. He was conscious of Melyna watching him from the bed, the erotic glaze slowly fading from her eyes. Then he heard the pad-pad-pad of bare feet on the floor, and felt two slender arms creeping around him from behind, two small hands creeping down toward his groin.

He laughed softly. "What, more?"

She laid her head against his back, and he felt her hair brush the base of his spine. He laughed again. "Really?"

The hands continued their downward motion and stopped in the obvious place. When they arrived there, they got the normal response.

Blade laughed a third time. "All right, Melyna. You want to get back into the habit, right?" There was a small murmur from behind him, which Blade took as a "Yes." Then he felt the hands on his body grasping him firmly by the hips and trying to turn him around. Blade chuckled deep in his throat and braced himself firmly. It would have taken a block and tackle to turn him around.

After a moment Melyna realized Blade wasn't going to move. So she did. With a quick wriggle she slipped under Blade's wide-spread legs, giving the insides of his thighs a playful pinch as she did. Another quick wriggle, and she was kneeling in front of Blade. Then her head thrust forward, like a bird darting at a particularly juicy worm. Her lips closed around Blade's half-awake erection. In a moment it was no longer just half-awake.

111

Eventually Blade and Melyna reached the point where they couldn't have conjured up a single erotic impulse between them if their lives had depended on it. Melyna used the rest of the water in the jug for her own washing, and together they went out into the morning.

It was just as well for Blade that he and Melyna got along so well—out of bed as well as in it. The next month was an ordeal of boredom and frustration for Blade.

It was not that the Councilors objected to Himgar's plans. They were more than willing to have Blade train the scouts in unarmed combat and help lead them down to the city. They were even willing to accept his proposal for the move north. But most of the people of the Purple River seemed to be doing nothing to get ready for the move.

Blade could understand their reluctance, and perhaps sympathize with it more than Himgar could. The War Councilor was a man with a mission. Like most such people, he was not overly willing to take into account mere human emotions in pursuing that mission.

Blade, on the other hand, was an outsider, a recent recruit to Himgar's projects. He could understand the people's fear of abandoning their homes and possessions. They would be striking out for a new and unknown land, where they might or might not be able to settle in peace. Finally, they would be making the new settlement with some of the women of the city of Brega. Himgar might see in the city and its learning the last hope of civilization in Brega. But for most of his followers, this was at best the lesser of two evils.

One of the most open doubters about Himgar's plan was also one of his staunchest supporters. Truja, the intended leader of the scouting party, had been a huntress of the city before Rilgon's Senar captured her a year ago. She hadn't even pretended to submit, so she had received the spread-eagling and the lash almost at once. By chance Truja had received barely a hundred lashes. So when they threw her out into the

112

forest to live or die, she had lived, and made her way to the Purple River lands. They had taken her in and healed her. At least they had healed her body, although from neck to buttocks her back was still one mass of ridged scars. Eventually Himgar had talked with her, and she had joined his band. Soon she had become leader of the scouts.

Truja was shorter than the other city women Blade had met, with a large-featured face and dark brown hair showing some streaks of gray. Her body was almost stocky, but well proportioned, and must have been quite desirable before the Senar whipman had left his marks on it. Now, however, Truja was altogether indifferent to her appearance. She was almost as indifferent to sex. Blade did notice, however, that Truja's eyes occasionally softened when they rested on Himgar. If Himgar had ever looked back . . . But the War Councilor lived with passion only for his mission.

Though Truja never shared Blade's bed, she would talk long and freely with him after the day's training. She had no use for any notion of trying to stay neutral in the coming war between Rilgon and the city.

"What we ought to do is send all the women and the children and the old men back into the forest, where Rilgon couldn't find them if he looked for a year. Then our fighters, and our fighters only, can march down to the city. They can meet with our sisters from the city, as Himgar wants. But then they should not simply march away. They should camp on the plains until Rilgon's army appears."

"And then?"

"Isn't it obvious, Blade? Rilgon's army will march on the city, and its fighting women will come out to meet the enemy. They will join in battle. And then we—we, with two thousand of the best fighting men and women in all the lands of Brega, we shall—"

"Take them in the rear?" Blade finished the sentence for her.

Truja smiled thinly and nodded. "Rilgon's mob of

113

killers will never get home if we do that. At least not enough of them to do any more harm. And the sisters of the city will think well of us, and perhaps give us understanding and aid that we could not get otherwise."

"Perhaps," said Blade pointedly.

Truja shrugged. "To be sure. I can promise nothing. But we shall get more that way than by following Himgar's plan. Even if we get nothing from the city, we will at least do more to Rilgon and his army of monsters." Insane rage flared in Truja's eyes as she said that. "But in the name of the Spirit of Union *and* Mother Kina, let us do *some*thing!"

Blade could not agree more with the last point. Summer was wearing on. Reports were coming up from the city of more and more bitter rivalry between the two factions, sometimes erupting into open violence. And equally disturbing reports were coming up from the Senar lands, reports that told of Rilgon's growing army. Each day its numbers and war skills increased. Is seemed likely that Rilgon would be able to lead out two thousand Blenar and ten times that many Senar. Even if all the fighting women of the city could unite to face Rilgon's invasion, they would have barely a quarter that many.

"What about the other women?" Blade asked Truja.

The scarred woman made a gesture of disgust. "They can no more fight than they can fly or lay eggs. Thank Mother Kina, most of the sisters who will be joining us are of the fighting classes. I doubt if most of the others could even survive the journey out of the city."

Blade wondered about that. In his travels in Dimension X he had seen some of the most unpromising people turn into formidable fighters in impossibly short periods of time. But that was a question for the future, when he had the walls of the city in sight. For the moment, he was here by the Purple River, and here he would stay until the people mustered up their courage to follow Himgar.

12.

Before Blade died of boredom or Himgar died of frustration, there was a compromise. The people would leave their homes. But only the fighting men and women would march down to the plains to meet the women coming out of the city. The others would head straight for the new lands, carrying with them whatever would be needed for the settlement there. Only a few fighters and some hunters would go with them, to guard against wild animals and hunt down game to feed the mass of people who would be making their way through the forest. Game would be abundant, and so would fish, roots and berries, and water. Another month, though, and this would not be so. Nor would it be good for the older people and the younger children to try crossing the passes in the mountains after the colder weather set in.

Himgar was far too happy that something was being done and in good time to quibble about the details. The moment the Council reached its decision, he came tearing down from the Council House and called the scouts together. He was so excited that he was jumping up and down like a child as he gave the scouts their orders.

"Now it doesn't matter if there is some argument over when the rest of the fighters leave. It doesn't matter at all. You people must leave at once and head for the city. You must get our friends out of the city —out of the city, I tell you. Rilgon may march any day. You must get there before his army does, and get the women out. You must!"

Blade noticed that Truja was looking at Himgar with the fond expression of a mother watching a brilliant son making his first public speech. When Himgar finally ran out of breath and things to say and left, Blade turned to the scarred woman.

"Did you have anything to do with this—change of plans, let's say?"

Truja shook her head. "Himgar has never paid any attention to me. And if he had, I certainly wouldn't have dared try to force him to change his mind about something. We would never get anywhere if I did that. No, I didn't do anything at all to get the plans changed." She paused. "Unless you count nightly prayers to both Mother Kina and the Spirit of Union."

The ten women and nine men of the scouting party moved out the next morning. Himgar saw them off, with more breathless exhortations and good wishes, and a deep regret that he could not go with them.

"Never mind," said Truja. "The fighters who will be coming after us need your leadership more than we do. The future of Brega depends more on them than on us."

There might have been more men in the scouting party. But the women, and only the women, could move freely about the city and the lands near it. The five women who came originally from the city itself would be the ones who actually slipped into it, to contact the friendly leaders.

Ten women, nine men—and one Senar. Nugun was desperately frightened for his master when he learned that Blade was going down among the women of the city. He flew into a fearsome rage when Truja tried to tell him that he could not go with Blade. And he was the happiest being in all of Brega when Blade finally persuaded Truja to let him go.

The trip through the forest and down into the plains was fast and uneventful. All of the scouts could cover twenty miles a day without even breathing hard, and there was plenty of food and water. Nor did they meet any enemies. Both roaming Senar and hunt-

116

ing parties from the city seemed to have abandoned the woods. As this became clear, Truja forced the pace to twenty-five and even thirty miles a day. They rose before dawn and seldom made camp much before darkness fell. It was as though everything depended on their pounding east as fast as their legs would carry them.

Perhaps it did.

They were through the forest in two days less than they had expected. On the western edge of the plains they stopped for a day and a night, waiting and watching. If the normal patrols from the city were roaming the plains, they would have to move slowly and carefully from here on. But if the feuds in the city actually made both factions unwilling to send their fighting women out of the city, the scouts might have an easy march.

Truja was a cheerful cynic about this, as she was about many things. "I'm quite sure the patrols won't be out," she said. "But we're certain to run into something else. A herd of stampeding cattle, a flash flood, a forest fire, a search for escaped males—our luck's bound to run out sooner or later."

But the patrols were thinner on the ground than usual, and there were no accidents. On the second morning they moved out onto the plains. More than a hundred miles farther east lay the city of Brega.

Moving by night and hiding to sleep by day, they covered more than two-thirds of that distance in less than four days. Blade was pleased to see Nugun earn the respect and trust of the other scouts during the night marches. The Senar's abnormally keen night vision guided the party through the darkness as fast as it could have moved by day. And more than once Nugun gave warning of the approach of night-prowling women in time to permit the scouts to go to ground.

None of these women were part of regular patrols or hunting parties. They were mostly small parties of two to six, flitting across the country as swiftly and

117

quietly as birds, intent on some private errand. Intrigue, assassination—who knew? None among the scouts did, and all were becoming increasingly curious, Blade most of all. Only Nugun was indifferent to the "higher" issues involved. His world was intensely physical and concrete—food, sex, war, marching, sleeping. The only abstract concept he could grasp was loyalty to Blade. The Englishman knew that the Senar would die slowly rather than betray him. He only hoped he could meet the same high standard if the matter came to a test.

For five days they crossed a land covered with patches of forest, small streams, pastures where single-horned blue-gray cattle grazed—and small farms. Blade crept close to one of those farms before the dew was off the grass one morning. The farm seemed to contain a dozen or so sturdy women, bare-legged in their short tunics and as brown as the rough cloth of those tunics. Much to Blade's surprise, the farm also held two men—captured Senar, judging from their hair and massive muscles. They seemed to be serving as domestic animals—hoisting water from the well, turning the grindstones, carrying huge loads of firewood.

Blade asked Truja about that when he returned to the scout camp. She shrugged. "Out here in the westlands the Laws of Mother Kina are not always followed strictly. There is much hard work in running a farm, and for much of it a man is stronger and cheaper than a draught animal. So not all of the Senar taken by the hunting parties end up on spits. Some end up on westland farms, and good coin or perhaps wine ends up in the hands of the huntresses."

After the fifth day, the farms became larger and there was less unused land between them. That meant more care was necessary in traveling, even by night, and much more care in choosing and concealing campsites. Here, barely forty miles from the city, the patrols still roamed fairly often. At least once a day the guards watching the nearest road would see a cloud of dust approaching. Shortly there would materialize under that dust cloud a score or so of heavily armed women, tramping along with dust-caked faces set and grim.

"There still aren't nearly as many as there would be if things were normal," said Truja. "The city is pulling in its horns. Rilgon will be able to take his men to within three days of the city with nothing but rumors running ahead of him." She looked grim.

To take Truja's mind off her forebodings of disaster, Blade changed the subject. "Shall we start looking for a point where the women fleeing from the city can meet? We ought to pick somewhere large enough to hold all the women but small enough to defend against attack. We'll have to deal with the women of the city and perhaps some of Rilgon's Senar if we can't get clear before they arrive."

Truja nodded wearily. "I know. But you're asking a lot. A plantation house would be the best. But even the abandoned ones are too close to the city to be very safe. And most of them are still in use. I doubt if we can find what you're looking for. We may have to find some forest and camp in the open."

But Truja's pessimism proved a poor guide. Blade and Nugun went out on patrol, and three days later they returned with broad smiles and a report of their find.

"It's a big, tall, sprawling thing, with five wings, built out of shiny black stone. Or at least it must have been shiny once," Blade added. "It's badly weathered and overgrown, but still sound inside."

"You went—inside?" said Truja, her mouth falling open so wide that Blade could barely understand her last word.

"Yes. Why not?"

"Black stone—that is—a War House of the people before the disaster. It is full of violence, evil, disease." She shuddered and sat down abruptly. "No. We will not use it."

"We shall indeed use it," said Blade. "I don't care what your city superstitions say. I know from my own

119

land that the worst evil of such a war would have passed away many generations ago. That War House will be perfectly safe. It—"

"But the violence left a curse, the men's—"

"Damn the violence and damn the curses and damn you for a superstitious idiot if you believe in either one!" Blade snapped. Some of the other scouts turned and stared at him. He reached down, seized Truja by the wrist, dragged her to her feet, then dragged her stumbling and protesting out of earshot of the rest of the scouts. He sat her down in the ferns and stood over her. There was an edge in his voice as he continued.

"The disaster was at least a thousand years ago. There is *no* way that War House can possibly still be dangerous. No diseases, nothing can survive that long. I know. I have seen such lingering deaths fade away in a single generation."

Truja nodded numbly, stunned into silence by his anger.

"And as for the rest—curses are something I didn't expect you to believe in. Not even curses from the disaster. I—"

"But the curse is from the violence of the men. They—"

"Balls! They weren't any more violent than the people today, men *or* women. Look at what's ripping the city apart. That silly quarrel that still has everybody so furious they won't cooperate in the face of an invasion. And the hunting parties' treatment of the Senar! Is that gentle, is that anything but violent? Curses!" Blade spat. "You women are just as bloody as the men from before the disaster. But if you believe in curses, you're a damned sight less civilized!" Blade turned angrily on his heel and strode away, to lean against a tree where he could quietly watch Truja.

She sat cross-legged on the grass for some time, her shoulders heaving with her indignant breathing. She was obviously deeply moved, and Blade could not help wondering if he had gone too far. But he knew that what he had said needed saying, whether gently or not.

Eventually Truja stopped holding her head stiffly erect, and let it sag down until her chin was on her chest. Blade noticed the sparkle of tears in the corner of dark eyes suddenly gone blank. He was tempted to go over to her and comfort her, but decided against it. She would have to work herself out of this mood and into whatever decision she would make without help from him.

It was hot even in the shade of the little grove, and Blade felt sweat starting out on his forehead and arms. Insects whined around his face, and he batted them away. The sound of cattle mooing reached him, carried on the breeze from far away.

Finally Truja sighed and stood up, turning toward Blade. She shook her head wearily. "Blade, I suppose you are right." Silence. "No, you *must* be right. I wish you were wrong. We have believed so much about the men, their violence. . . ." Her voice broke for a moment. "We were blind to our own. I almost wish I were still blind. It—it does not feel very good."

Blade shrugged. "I did not say what I did because I wanted to hurt you."

"I know. But—I think you had better lead us now. I—I do not really know what is right and what is wrong any more. And that is not a state of mind for a leader," she ended, with a flash of her old spirit.

"All right," said Blade slowly. "If you want me to—"

"I do. Very much." For a moment her hand reached out and groped blindly, then found his. Her fingers closed on his with a firm, hard pressure. Then her hand dropped to her side.

"Come on, let's go back to the others. They will be thinking we're making love on the grass."

Blade raised an eyebrow, and Truja shook her head hastily, laughing. "No, Blade. Not now, not for a time. Perhaps . . . But then there is Himgar." She shook her head and turned away.

With Truja's doubts resolved, the scouting party broke camp that night when the light was barely out of the sky. Driving hard through the darkness, they reached the War House well before dawn. They saw it looming out of the forest, towering a hundred feet high and spreading five times that wide, vast, black, and sinister. Even the Purple River scouts, less aware of the legends of the disaster, hung back at first.

Blade and Truja set the doubts more or less at rest by walking into the house side by side and then out again half an hour later. They were dusty but unharmed. Assembling everyone in the gloom of the ground floor, Truja handed over her leadership to Blade. The cheers that rose into the darkness made it obvious that Blade was a more than acceptable choice.

That was well and good, but there was much more that needed to be done before the old War House was a fit refuge. A certain number of rooms had to be cleared of dust, mold, spider webs, bird's nests, and the remains of long-dead animals. A nearby spring had to be found. A regular roster of guards had to be set, and much else.

The house was a good ten miles from the nearest farm, so they could do much of this by daylight. Before darkness fell again, the scouts were as settled in as they could be. Blade and Truja went out into the twilight and sat down to plan the next move.

"The women who are going to the city must leave soon," said Truja. "There is no time to waste in getting them out of the way of Rilgon. He may march any day."

Blade nodded. "The rest of us will keep our heads down until the women start coming out from the city. It won't help if the patrols find out that we're here."

Truja laughed. "That's putting it mildly. But there is one thing you can do. I don't know if there's any game in this forest, so it might be wise to take a look at the local farms. I know some of them around here have fishponds and poultry runs, where a few people could snatch a good bit of meat."

Blade nodded. "But what about guards?"

"The farms this close to the city are seldom well guarded. What do they have to fear? Or at least—what *did* they have to fear?"

The idea of a little quiet chicken stealing was a good one. Or at least it might have been a good one, if Truja had been right about the guards at the farms. But there were supposed to be a number of escaped slaves roaming the area, so the farmers had taken precautions. And when Blade and Nugun came slipping up to a farm in the darkness, they ran into those precautions.

When dawn broke the next day, neither Blade nor Nugun had returned to the camp in the War House, Truja paced up and down, face grim, wondering what could have happened to them, fearing the worst.

She was almost right. Blade and Nugun were both lying on the bottom of a deadfall pit at the edge of the nearest farm. There were no stakes in the bottom of the pit, so neither had impaled himself like a fowl on a spit. But both were bruised, battered, and in no shape at all to fight the score or so of armed women who ringed the edges of the pit. The women stared down and occasionally brandished their scythes, hoes, and clubs. Blade stared back up at them and occasionally made a rude gesture.

He felt rather disgusted with himself.

13

Blade felt even more disgusted with the women than he did with himself. But he kept his mouth shut.

Nugun didn't, however. He beat his chest and jumped up and down. He bellowed and roared and cursed and screamed. He even snatched up clods of earth from the sides of the pit and hurled them up at the women standing around the edge. One clod hit hard. The woman clapped a hand to her arm and swore back at Nugun. The women on either side of her raised their scythes and glared down.

Blade realized that Nugun's rage was likely to get both of them killed outright.

"Nugun!"

The Senar spun around, with another clod raised in one massive hand.

"Blade?"

"Nugun, stop that at once!"

"But women, they—"

"I said *stop it!*"

Nugun grunted a reluctant agreement and let the clod drop. Blade could see the women above relax.

A thick rope snaked down over the edge of the pit. Blade walked over to it and found that it would hold his weight. Slowly he began to climb, hand over hand, looking up occasionally. If the women above were just a little careless when he reached the top . . .

But as he crawled out on the edge of the pit, the women stepped back, holding their tools in front of them. As Blade rose to his feet, three of them ran forward, carrying a tight-meshed net of heavy rope, with stones tied around its edges. The net soared into the air and came down on top of him, weighing him down until he could barely lift his arms.

A bellow from below told of another burst of rage from Nugun. Blade turned and saw the Senar swarming up the rope like a maddened ape. As his massive head burst over the edge of the pit, one of the women stepped close to Blade and thrust a knife against his ribs. Then she shouted over her shoulder to Nugun:

"You fight—he dies."

The knife pricked Blade's ribs. He felt blood ooze out and trickle down. He held his breath, half mad with rage and helpless frustration. He wasn't quite sure that he wanted Nugun to stop.

But again Nugun grunted agreement, climbed out onto the edge of the pit, and stood up, arms at his sides. He stood there tamely as another net was thrown over him. His expression did not change even when one of the women stepped behind him with a stout club and brought it down full force on his head. Blade let out a roar of fury, but Nugun simply sagged down, dragging the three women off their feet. Blade could not help laughing at their struggles to untangle themselves from the net. He was still laughing when the other women led him away.

As the women marched Blade to the farmhouse, it was obvious that they weren't quite sure what to make of him. He could not possibly be an escaped Senar slave—he wasn't hairy or brawny enough. Breeding Males never left the House of Fertility—the guardians saw to that. And Blade couldn't possibly be female. So what was he?

When they reached the house, the women led Blade around to a shed out in back and locked him in. The last words he heard from his captors as they drifted away was a suggestion to ask the patrol the next time it came by.

Alone in the smelly and bug-ridden darkness, Blade considered his situation. There was a piece of good news in the women's words. They had no idea that

125

people from the mountains might be prowling in the plains. So Blade wouldn't have to answer questions on the subject—or undergo torture for refusing to answer them.

But where was Nugun, and what had they done with him? Had they killed the Senar outright, or were they going to make him another farm slave? Blade suspected that Nugun would rather die than be a woman's slave. And left to himself, Nugun would certainly be able to goad the women into killing him sooner or later. Blade knew that the only thing he could do for the Senar was to escape before the patrol arrived and release Nugun.

But there was no hope of escaping during the remaining daylight hours. Blade went over to the door and tested the lock. The rattle made the woman on guard outside turn and glower at him through the narrow slit in the heavy wood. He thumbed his nose at her and stepped back. The lock couldn't be broken, but the guard might be persuaded to open it. When darkness fell . . .

In the meantime, get some sleep. Blade lay down on the floor and made himself as comfortable as the hard dirt permitted. The lowing of cattle in a nearby corral was the last thing he heard as he drifted off to sleep.

Blade awoke to see that it was night outside, but not dark. Several torches sent flickering light through the cracks in the walls and the slit in the door. Blade could hear the sound of footsteps all around the hut and numerous voices, chattering like a whole cageful of birds.

Blade's eyes wandered across the floor of the hut. He started as he saw Nugun lying there, feet bound and hands tied behind his back. A massive crust of blood marred one side of his huge head.

Blade rose to his feet and was starting toward the Senar when the door of the hut opened with a rattle of chains and bolts. Blade spun around with a momentary notion of jumping the first woman who came through the door and snatching her weapons. Then he

126

realized that even if he escaped now, he could only do so by abandoning Nugun. He would not do that. There would be other times.

The first four women to step through the door were all warriors in patrol uniforms. Two had drawn swords thrust out in front of them; the others carried strung bows with arrows nocked to them. The archers moved into opposite corners of the hunt, their arrows pointed at Blade. The swordswomen took positions on either side of the door. Then the patrol leader stepped into the hut.

Blade could not keep his jaw from falling open for a second in sheer astonishment. The patrol leader was the leader of the hunting party Blade had attacked in the forest! He got his mouth closed as soon as she recognized him, and her mouth opened in turn.

After a moment she grinned, white teeth snapping together. "Ah, the strange man of the forest. I have been wondering who you were and where you might have gone. Well, there is only one place you are going now. The arena of the city will have such a spectacle as never before, when you die there." Then she turned on her heel, walked outside, and began shouting orders to the rest of the patrol and cursing the farm women for their slowness.

Lashed on by the tall woman's orders, the farm women pushed and shoved Blade out of the hut. They tied his hands and forced him into the back of a heavy wagon drawn by six of the blue-gray cattle. Then they brought Nugun out, still unconscious. They carried him up to the wagon and threw him into the straw in the bottom like a sack of grain. Blade glared down at the women, but they merely glared back and made obscene gestures at him.

The patrol leader climbed up on the seat of the wagon beside the driver and snapped out an order. With whip-crackings and shouts from the driver, the cart began to move, and the patrol fell in on either side of it. Sitting beside Nugun, helpless to do anything for him, Blade watched the farm recede into the darkness.

The wagon and its escort kept moving until the sky began to turn gray. Then the tall woman ordered a halt and let her fighters scatter into the fields. Some simply sagged down onto the ground and took off their boots and helmets; others broke out cheese and coarse bread and nibbled at that. The tall leader climbed down from the wagon and walked around and around it. She neither ate nor drank, and her dust-caked face was as set and expressionless as if it had been made of iron.

Half an hour later the leader lined up her women, and the squeal and grind of the wagon wheels began again. This time it kept on all day. By the time the sun was low in the sky, all the women looked like dusty ghosts as they plodded along, putting one aching foot painfully in front of the other. Their eyes were sullen as they stared at their leader, riding almost in comfort beside the wagon driver. But Blade could see the leader's face better than the others. Something was twisting it from within, something even beyond fatigue. Blade did not like being in the power of such a driven woman.

Before the sun dropped completely below the horizon, the wagon turned aside into a flat, hard field rimmed by a line of squat, bushy trees. There was not a breath of wind to move a leaf on the trees or a blade of the long brown-green grass. With the sweat drying on his body, Blade watched the women pitch heavy leather tents and dig fire pits.

Beside Blade, Nugun also watched the women bustling about. The Senar had regained consciousness just before noon. But he had said nothing, either to Blade or to the women. Blade hoped Nugun was simply pretending to submit, following his master's apparent lead.

After making camp, the women turned to Blade and Nugun. They dragged the Senar out, cut the ropes at his wrists and ankles, and spread-eagled him between

128

four posts driven into the ground. Blade watched the spectacle with a sinking feeling in his stomach. Were they going to abuse Nugun and eat him, the way they had dealt with his comrades in the forest?

Apparently not. After staking Nugun out, most of the women wandered off toward the trees. Some of them pulled off their tunics as they walked, and their bare breasts swayed gently, gleaming in the fading light. Two who remained by the cart drew their swords and motioned Blade to dismount. He unstretched cramped legs and let the women urge him toward a tent smaller than the others and well apart from them. The women led him up to the front of the tent and motioned for him to enter. Then they cut the cords binding his hands.

When he did so, he was not surprised to find the patrol leader inside, sitting cross-legged on a cushion in the back of the tent. A candle in a metal holder cast a pale yellow light on her taut face. It creased in a brief smile as she saw Blade enter. The smile widened as she saw Blade's eyes roaming the tent, looking for any sign of weapons within her reach—or his. She drew a knife from under the cushion and placed it on one well-rounded thigh. "I have this. But you are strong and quick, and no doubt could overpower me in spite of it. However, you seem to care for that filthy beast out there. Are you one of those men from the legends, who could love only other men?"

Blade managed to keep his face straight. "No. He is my sworn follower, who has come into danger out of his loyalty to me."

"An odd attitude for one of the beast-men to show, I must say."

"Perhaps you find it odd because there is no loyalty in the city?"

The woman's smile faded for a moment. "Do not try to play word games with me, warrior. I am Idrana, huntress *and* warrior of the city, Sworn Sister of the Greens. If I give the word, or if any harm comes to me—that 'follower' of yours dies as the Senar usually do at our hands. Is that clear?"

Blade nodded.

"Good. Now we can talk and perhaps make sense. I—" Idrana broke off as footsteps sounded outside. The flap behind Blade opened, and two of the women pushed a dripping leather skin of water into the tent. They showed signs of wanting to linger, but Idrana fixed them with a poisonous glare and they backed out hastily. Blade could not help thinking that Idrana was remarkably careless of the good will of her patrol. Blade had known armies in which an officer would wind up with a sword through his ribs for less than he had seen Idrana do today. As Idrana started pulling her tunic over her head, he said so.

Idrana finished pulling off the tunic and sat there bare to the waist for a moment, staring at Blade. Then she laughed and reached for the waterskin. "It is nothing for me to worry about. They are all Sisters of the Greens with me now, and they know they will be well rewarded."

Idrana seemed in a conversational mood, so Blade decided to venture another question. "Rewarded? How?"

Idrana lifted the waterskin and poured some water from it over her shoulders and breasts. It ran down, making streaks in the dust on her tanned skin. A drop formed at the end of each solid, dark nipple, then fell off as her breasts moved.

"Soon the Greens will find a way to choose the new Mistress of Fertility. When they have done that, I will be chief warrior of those guarding the House. It is a highly honorable post for a fighting woman of the city, one that women have killed for in the past."

"And I suppose they are planning to kill for it in the future?"

Idrana's hands were now scrubbing the grime from her face and neck. She stiffened for a moment. Then her tight smile was back. "So you do know what is going on in the city. I wonder how." Idrana shook

130

her head to get the water out of her ears and unbuckled the belt of her trousers, shoving them down her long legs. Blade found it getting harder by the minute to keep his eyes on Idrana's face.

When she was completely nude she shrugged, giving her breasts an interesting motion. Then she said, "I don't suppose you really know all the details. And if you don't know any of the secrets of the Greens, you couldn't have done any damage."

Blade decided that it was time to say soemthing. If he went on sitting there like a log, Idrana might get the wrong idea. "I barely knew who the Greens were before you told me, Idrana."

"Indeed?" she said. She was pouring water down between her thighs now. The droplets sparkled and gleamed on the mass of brown-black curls between her legs. "Well, you know now. And you will know more about them in time. But first—you will know more about me, and I about you." She poured the rest of the water down her legs and stood up, nude and gleaming. "You are a most unusual specimen of man, warrior. But I cannot go on calling you—warrior. Have you a name?"

"Blade."

"Then come here, Blade, that we can learn more about each other." She crooked a finger at him in a gesture that might have been coy with another woman. With Idrana, it was as commanding as a drill sergeant's bellowed order.

Blade stood up. He could not have pretended not to be aroused if he had wanted to. Idrana's slow stripping, uncaring or unaware of what it was doing to him, had given him a good start. He stepped toward her, and she met him halfway. A long, muscular, warm body flowed up against him, and her lips rose up to his, warm and wet and seeming to suck resistance out of him.

He stood still as sure, powerful hands went down to his belt, unbuckled it, unlaced his trousers, and slipped in under their waistband. Under the trousers he was wearing only a breechcloth. A quick ripping of cloth, and the dance of warm fingers on his stiffening maleness began. Meanwhile the warm lips left his and began to work down, nuzzling his chin and throat.

When her lips fell on the filthy homespun of Blade's tunic, Idrana stopped for a moment. She practically tore it off his back. When he was as nude as she was, she started in again with fingers and lips and warm flesh pressing against him. They all worked very well, and as they did, Idrana was obviously arousing herself along with Blade. Not as fast—he was almost painfully aroused before her breathing quickened. But just as surely. In time her breasts were heaving, just as his chest was, and her nipples were standing as stiff and erect as he was.

It was then that she took him by the shoulders and pushed him down. With another woman Blade would have resisted for a moment, making a game of it. But Idrana did not play games—this was obvious. Blade let himself bend back until he could lower himself to the ground. Then his hands went around behind Idrana, ran quickly and lightly down the long, straight back, and clasped the firm buttocks as hard as possible. He was damned if he was going to give this woman complete control! His grip tightened. Idrana gasped—and then Blade pulled Idrana down onto him.

Her face contorted in the moment of penetration, but not in pain. She was already wet and getting wetter as Blade thrust up into her and began rocking his hips back and forth. Perhaps Idrana's plans had been to set the pace herself. But Blade had snatched the initiative back for himself. He held her too tight and moved too strongly for her to do anything about it. Before she could fight back, her will began to dissolve under the impact of Blade's thrusting. Her head went back; her mouth sagged open in an idiotic gape. Sometimes her eyes closed tight, as Blade rose up high and deep. At other times they opened wide and stared unbelievingly down at him. It was something beyond Idrana's experience and perhaps beyond her belief—a man taking

132

the initiative, slowly and deliberately melting her down into an erotic mass.

Blade was aware of sweat rolling from his own body. He was even more aware of how close he was to the limits of his own endurance. But he went on and on until he felt that the woman above him was tightened like a bowstring ready for release. Her back was arched, and her hands were clutching his shoulders so tightly that her nails dug into his flesh.

Then the bowstring was released, and Idrana's back arched still further, until Blade wondered if her spine were going to snap. She bounced up and down and twisted from side to side like a puppet on strings, whimpering and sobbing and gulping air. Then she slumped forward until her nipples brushed his chest. The sudden shift of position put an end to Blade's endurance. Now it was his turn to heave and twist and groan as he burst upward into her.

Eventually the mindless erotic fog faded away for both of them. Idrana rolled off Blade and sprawled limply beside him. By what was obviously a heroic effort of will, she managed to be the first to get to her feet and call for food and more water.

After a meal of bread and cheese and dried meat washed down with water, Idrana gave Blade the explanation she had promised. Most of it Blade could have guessed from what she had already said. The Greens and the Blues were the factions in the city competing to choose the next Mistress of the House of Fertility. Matters had become so tense that the Greens were planning open violence.

"And no doubt the Blues also," said Idrana. "But we will be striking first. Three weeks from now, there will be the Great Games in the arena. No woman who can be there will be elsewhere, and that includes the leaders of the Blues."

Blade nodded. "And then the Sworn Sisters of the Greens will—act?"

"Yes. With their leaders—gone—the Blues will not dare submit a candidate for mistress. Ours will win

133

easily, and then I will be appointed warrior of the House of Fertility, to guard it and its secrets." She paused, with what could only be called a smug grin on her face.

Then she lowered her voice and said, "I will be in a good position to reward those who help me. And I may rise higher yet. First Warrior of the city, perhaps. Then no one can say a word against what I do. I I could even keep—a man."

Blade nodded. "And you want me to be that man?"

Idrana smiled. "Of course. The women are not bad, and the Senar are good for variety. But a real man—like something out of legend—I will be the most envied woman in the city."

And the most hated, thought Blade. But that was better left unsaid. For a moment he was silent. Obviously there was nothing in this offer that he needed to take seriously. Idrana was about as trustworthy as a cobra. And even if she was sincere, she was trying to enlist him in the faction fighting in the city. The faction fighting that could do nothing for the city except lay it open to Rilgon's army.

But for the moment, Idrana might be offering a milder captivity, one affording more opportunity to contact the "sisters" in the city, more chance to escape —and a chance to protect Nugun.

Blade made his decision. "All right. You interest me. And you will have power in the city. But I will only aid you on one condition. Release the Senar Nugun to me. Or better yet, set him free entirely."

If Blade had thrust a white-hot iron into her, Idrana could not have started more violently. Her face went pale, then contorted into an ugly mask. "Blade, are you joking?"

"No—why should I be?"

"Set free—one of those—animals? Treat it like—something human? Never! The Senar will die in the arena as part of the games, and that is all there is to it."

Blade's temper flared. "Animals, are they? Then you women of the city have strange tastes in sex. I saw

134

what you did with those Senar in the forest—animal-lover!"

In the next moment Blade knew that his temper had definitely taken him too far. Idrana screamed like a wounded animal and snatched her knife from the corner of the tent. She raised it in one trembling hand and held it over Blade's groin, lowering it slowly. Blade lay still, not moving a muscle. If she stayed blinded by rage, when her knife hand came within reach of a quick grab—

But Idrana's scream had alerted the women outside. The tent flap flew open, and Blade found himself staring at the shimmering metal of three drawn swords. No matter what he did, at least one of them would drive into his neck before he could move. So he went on lying still, not an easy thing with the knife still dropping lower and lower, the point now aimed directly at his groin.

But Idrana's rage passed before the steel drove into Blade's flesh. The knife flashed in the candlelight as she threw it across the tent and leaped to her feet, still naked and quivering all over with rage.

"Take him out and spread-eagle him!" she snarled. "If he loves that Senar so much, he can spend the night the same way. And he can die the same way in the arena, and think about what he missed! Oh, Mother Kina!" Idrana spat hard in Blade's face, then turned away and slumped to the ground, her shoulders heaving.

As the women dragged him to his feet and out of the tent, Blade could not help wondering if he had done the wisest thing. But—face it—the only alternative would have been abandoning Nugun to death in the arena. That he could not have done. Now they would be in the arena together—and where one alone might die, two together might contrive to live.

14

In two days they reached the city of Brega. By Idrana's orders, Blade was spread-eagled each night and bullied and harassed during the day. Idrana was obviously still in a fine blaze of rage and frustration with him.

So Blade's eyes burned and his muscles ached as he watched the city grow larger in the dawn. It made him think of the skeleton of a giant.

Once the city must have covered many times its present area. Among the fields and farms beside the road were numerous piles of crumbling stone. The farmhouses and fences themselves had been put together from salvaged stone. The present city was almost a village in comparison with its departed ancestor. It lurked behind a low wall of roughly mortared stone and a narrow ditch filled with scummy water. The smell of that water reached Blade's nostrils when the wagon was still a mile from the wall.

"You women are certainly sloppy housekeepers," he said to Idrana. "I've known barnyards that smelled sweeter than your beloved city."

Idrana's dusty face twisted in a sneer. "Go on taunting us, Blade. Let your tongue wag if you wish, until it is silent forever."

"That may be longer than you think, woman," said Blade calmly.

The women of the patrol dropped behind the wagon as it came up to the walls and followed it through the gate. Neither the gate nor the wall impressed Blade very much. Both were pieced together out of timber

136

and salvaged stone and metal. Neither would offer much of an obstacle to an attacker. And the ditch was solid earth in several places. If Rilgon had the foresight to prepare ladders or even prop logs against the wall, he could put a thousand men into the city in a few minutes.

Inside the walls, things might not be so easy for an attacker who did not know the city. The streets were narrow and wound back and forth and up and down like drunken snakes. The close-packed houses offered infinite opportunities for ambushes and sniping by the archers. But to balance this, they were mostly built of wood. A small fire, a strong wind—and the women of the city would die in its ashes. If the fighting women of the city had any sense, they would march out and try to meet Rilgon in the open field. To stay in their city would be laying their necks on the block and begging for Rilgon to swing the axe.

Not all of the city was a rat's nest of wooden houses. A mile away on the right, a gigantic black stone mass rose high above the shingled roofs and rough stone chimneys. It looked like an enormous arcade, with a fringe of brightly colored banners fluttering from poles on top and massive arches below.

Idrana saw Blade's eyes resting on the arcade. "The arena, Blade—the place of your death. Look your fill on it today. You will be too busy to admire it the next time you see it."

"I do indeed admire it," said Blade with a thin smile. "It is the only thing I can admire in this 'city' that hardly deserves the name. What wretched builders you women seem to be. No doubt the arena is left over from the era of men, before the disaster."

The thrust went home. Idrana's nostrils flared, and her knuckles went white as her hand tightened on the hilt of her dagger. Blade tensed, but Idrana got her temper under control again. She sat in grim silence, swaying slightly as the wagon bumped and jolted over ruts and potholes in the half-paved streets. Blade relaxed and looked around again.

The arena was not the only building in the city that obviously went back to before the disaster. Two miles away on the left rose a gigantic square tower, a monstrous black mass at least half a mile on a side and a thousand feet high. There were no banners on it, no windows or arches in it. Far down at the bottom, Blade could see a large door, metallic silver against the blackness, with a broad wooden staircase painted yellow leading up to it. Nothing else relieved the solid blackness.

Again Idrana noticed where Blade was looking. This time her voice was full of pride as she said, "The House of Fertility. From its secrets, the city rose and will rise farther yet."

Blade nodded without replying. So that mighty black mass housed the secrets of the city's ability to reproduce? Blade had no doubt that the secrets existed. He had heard so from too many people.

But what were they? He suspected that the people of the disaster had been particularly skilled in biology and chemistry. The legends of bacteriological and chemical warfare in the disaster suggested as much. But what exactly had they learned to do? Had they achieved one of the longstanding dreams of Home Dimension scientists—developing embryos from fertilized eggs in laboratories? Or was their "secret" even more fantastic, something for which Home Dimension lacked even the words? Blade wondered. His curiosity was aroused, and once it was aroused, it seldom went back to sleep. He would ferret out the answer, somehow, sooner or later—if he lived long enough.

A few minutes later the wagon and the patrol turned into a muddy courtyard. Around three sides of the courtyard rose a five-story wooden building, with "barracks" stamped all over it. Armed women were drifting in and out of the door, and more were staring down from the windows at the new arrival. If they were going to imprison him here, in the middle of what looked like half the city's fighting women, Blade knew his chances of escape would be slim.

They were. Eight of the brawniest women Blade had ever seen came tramping up to the wagon. Idrana said nothing, merely jerked her thumb over her shoulder at Blade and Nugun. Four of the women scrambled up into the wagon and picked up Nugun as though he had been a log. The Senar growled deep in his throat and glared around him, but did not try to wriggle or fight. Blade had impressed that on him during the trip—don't provoke the women into killing you, no matter what they do. Stay alive and wait until we're together—that's our best chance for escape. I will not leave you.

"Good luck, Nugun," called Blade, as the women hauled the Senar away. Idrana glared at him; then the other women were picking him up and lugging him away too. He followed his own advice and did not struggle or swear. But it was a considerable temptation when the women banged him against doorposts and walls in their haste or carelessness.

Quite a few bruises later, they reached the bottom of a flight of stone stairs. Ahead stretched a long corridor, floored and walled with slimy stones. A few oil lamps on iron brackets gave off a sullen yellow light and greasy smoke. the air lay heavy on Blade's nostrils, damp and chill and reeking of mold and long-confined humanity.

Cells opened onto the corridor on either side. As the women carried him past, Blade could see huddled, wretched figures in most of them. Some were men, mostly Senar. Some were women, and some were so gaunt and ragged that it was impossible to tell what they were.

Finally an empty cell appeared on the left. The women tramped into it, dropped Blade with a thump into several inches of moldy straw, cut his bonds, and marched out. As they did, Blade saw the leader making complicated signs with her fingers to the other three. He realized then why the four women had said nothing, and why Idrana had commanded them with gestures. They were deaf-mutes!

139

It was two days before anybody even bothered to bring Blade food and water. When they did, the food was a loaf of sour, barely edible bread. The water was gray and scummy-looking, as if it might have been dipped out of the ditch around the city's walls. It tasted as bad. But Blade realized he had no alternative —he had to eat and drink what they gave him, or lose strength even more rapidly than he would otherwise. If he lost too much strength, escape would be impossible, even if he found an opportunity. He ate and drank.

He ate the sour bread and drank the murky water for ten days. Twice the guards brought in fresh straw and a bucket of almost-clean water for him to wash himself. But his hair and beard grew and became a tangled mess, and he could feel himself losing strength day by day. To keep his muscles in tone and his reflexes sharp, he did a series of exercises each day. The exercises made his blood race and his breath come faster and gave him at least a moment's illusion of continued health and vitality.

But it was only an illusion. It was obvious that nobody really cared about keeping him in shape to put on a good show in the arena. Or perhaps they were doing this deliberately, fearing that he would try to escape if he retained his strength.

But this hardly made sense. The bars of his cell were too strong and too solidly set to be broken or bent out. The guards who brought him his food and water were always on the alert, standing well back with drawn swords. At most, he could take one or two of them with him. Even if he was incredibly lucky in the cell, he would hardly be so lucky everywhere along the route to the open air. And it would be a miracle pure and simple if he were able both to fight off the guards *and* find Nugun.

Eleven days, twelve, thirteen. The morning of the fourteenth day came. Blade scratched the fourteenth mark on the wall and settled down to his "breakfast."

The loaf of bread seemed even more battered and misshapen than usual. It looked as though someone had been using it for a punching bag before sending it down to him. He ripped the heel off the loaf and began to munch on it wearily. Apart from all its other faults, the bread was so hard that it was making Blade's gums raw and sore.

Suddenly his teeth came together on something so hard that it made him start and wince. Carefully he worked thumb and forefinger in between his teeth, grasped the object, and pulled it out.

It was a nut—a plain, ordinary black nut, of a kind that he had seen growing wild in the forests of Brega a dozen times. But it was an unexpected thing to find in a loaf of ration bread. Did it mean anything except that the bakers were careless?

It probably didn't, but he couldn't be sure. Blade waited until none of the guards were within earshot. Then he hurled the nut against the wall as hard as he could. There was a sharp *crack*. He went over to pick it up, found a hairline split in one half of the shell, and used his fingernails to pry it apart.

A small piece of paper fluttered out. Blade grabbed it out of the air before it could hit the straw, shielded it with his body, and read:

> Blade. Wait for day of Great Games in arena. Plans to rescue you made. Fighters of Purple River and army of Rilgon both entering plains. Our sisters already leaving city.
>
> Truja

The handwriting and signature were unmistakable. Blade read the note over several times until he was sure he had memorized it. Then he tore it up and swallowed the fragments.

So Truja was in the city and working to get him out. Hopefully Nugun was there too, although the

141

Senar was not mentioned in the note. Well and good—or at least well and better than anything he might be able to manage on his own. He would follow Truja's request for that reason—and that reason only.

15

Truja's plan was the best prospect Blade had, but not at all foolproof. With both Rilgon's army and the Purple River force on the march, someone might warn the city any day. Not likely, but not impossible either. If that happened, the Great Games would be canceled. And then the best opportunity for rescuing Blade would vanish.

Possibly Truja was bold enough to risk snatching Blade from the prison below the barracks. But unless Truja's raiders were strong or the guards distracted, the operation would be suicidal.

Blade sighed. For the week remaining until the games, his safety depended more on the undetected advance of Rilgon's army than on anything Truja or any other friends of his could do. Blade believed in luck—but as a professional, he hated like the plague to depend on it this much.

For the remaining week of his captivity, Blade's biggest problem was not to seem too eager for the day of the games to arrive. Even the least observant guard would start wondering why a man was so enthusiastic about the day of his death.

For the evening meal on the last day, they brought Blade an immense platter of meat that was raw on the inside and charred black on the outside. As much as he wanted to gorge himself, he ate only a few slices. He did not want to be slow and sluggish from too much food tomorrow morning when he entered the arena.

The guards came for him early the next morning,

binding his hands but leaving his feet free. Then they marched him briskly down the corridor and up the stairs to the courtyard of the barracks.

It was a bright day outside. After so many weeks of darkness the sun dazzled Blade. For his first few steps he had to grope his way forward, feeling for solid ground underfoot. Raucous laughter from all around the courtyard accompanied his fumblings.

Now Blade thought he understood why he had been ill-fed and ill-treated, left unwashed and unshaven and generally degraded. The ruling women of the city *had* to degrade a civilized man if they captured him. Otherwise those who saw him might begin to wonder if men might be worth more than the Laws of Mother Kina said. And if they began to wonder about that . . .

But understanding the reason for his treatment didn't make Blade appreciate it any more. His mood was savage as the women tied a rope around his neck and led him out of the courtyard like a prize steer. Once out in the street, they broke into a jog. They were obviously trying to wear Blade down and make him fall pitifully to the street. But his exercises in his cell had kept his muscles in better shape than the women had expected. His legs were aching and his breath burning in his chest and throat, but he was still on his feet when he reached the arena.

It loomed monstrous and black above him. The roar of the crowd from inside suggested that half the population of the city must be there already. And more were coming in each minute, most on foot, some in wagons, a few brought in on curtained litters. Several of the litters were festooned with brightly colored banners, blue and green. Even more of the banners flew from poles on the rim of the arena, so that it looked as though it had blossomed out in flowers.

That was all Blade had a chance to see before his guards hustled him through a small door near the base of the arena. Inside, a dark, dank corridor led steeply down, ending in a heavy polished metal door. One of the guards banged on it with the hilt of her sword, and it rumbled open.

Inside, the crowd roar came even louder from above, broken by occasional bursts of cheers and groans. Apparently the preliminaries to the games were already well underway. Working up the crowd's blood lust, Blade thought. He looked around the vaulted chamber, searching for a familiar face, searching above all for Nugun. But the Senar was nowhere in sight.

In the corner of the chamber stood a large, wheeled cage holding four Senar. They were even filthier than usual for the breed and were growling savagely and clawing at the bars of their cage. Chained to the wall just out of their reach was a nude girl, sitting slumped in total dejection and despair. Some lawbreaker, no doubt, tried and condemned to be thrown to the Senar in the arena. And the Senar would doubtless have been drugged or beaten to make them savage enough to put on a proper show for the bloodthirsty crowd in the stands. Blade wondered if he would get the same treatment or if they thought he would be nasty enough in his normal state. If they thought the latter, they were right. In his present mood, he would have torn any of the warriors of the city limb from limb, barehanded and without a qualm. Chivalry be damned!

Blade turned as the door rumbled open again and saw Idrana stalk in, followed by a file of armed women. By the time the door closed behind them, there were more than fifty packed into the chamber. Blade noticed that all carried bows and *very* well-filled quivers.

The women arranged themselves around the chamber, keeping close to the walls and leaving an open space in the middle for Blade and his guards. They seemed reluctant to approach him, as though he were a wild animal. Or perhaps they sensed the fury that was bubbling in him and feared it might suddenly boil over onto them.

Idrana had no such fear. She stepped up to Blade

145

until she was close enough to reach out and touch him. Her nostrils flared at his odor. Otherwise she seemed poised and ready, like an arrow about to fly from the bow. Blade decided against taunting her. She looked able to kill him on the spot, even if it spoiled part of her show.

"You look worried, Blade. Is it that you do not know what will be done with you?" Blade made no reply, and after a moment Idrana realized that he would make none. She grinned.

"You—you and your friend the Senar—will be taken to the center of the arena. My women and I will stand around the edge of the arena with our bows. And we will shoot arrows at you. We will try not to hit you—at first. We want good sport, and the good sight of men—*men*—running about like bugs from a fire, while our arrows whistle past their ears. And then, when we have put so many arrows into you that you look like spinefruit, we—" She broke off abruptly, as though she had suddenly realized she might be about to say too much.

Blade carefully kept his face expressionless, but inside he was a churning mass of thoughts. Nugun was alive—for the moment. And they were both going to be shoved out to die as—*archery targets*—to put on a show for the city.

A final roar of cheers and shouts came from up above. It died away, and in the silence that followed Blade heard drums roll and a single trumpet call out, high and brassy. Idrana spoke to Blade's guards. "Lead him out," she said briskly.

As she spoke, the gate to the arena itself rumbled open. Blade stared out across two hundred yards of hard-packed sand. It was bare and featureless with only a few patches of blood here and there. On it nothing moved, except a two-wheeled cart drawn by an ambling ox. The cart was piled high with the bodies of Senar. Blade saw arms and legs trailing down.

Then the trumpet sounded again, and Blade's guards

pulled him out into the sunlight. He blinked—and then stiffened as he saw another door open in the wall of the arena. Eight guards emerged, pulling a wheeled cage. In that cage was a single Senar.

Nugun.

Blade did not realize that he had shouted the name aloud. Idrana bared even white teeth in a savage grin as she heard him. "So he is—something unnatural—to you after all? Well, well. It is said that such pairs have a great desire to die together. At least you cannot deny that we have granted you that wish."

If Idrana had spoken three more words, Blade would have strangled her on the spot. But she said nothing, and the rope tightened around his neck as the guards stepped up their pace.

Five minutes later he stood in the very center of the arena. Twenty feet away stood Nugun, staring at Blade as though he were someone returned from the dead. Perhaps to the Senar he was.

Blade raised a hand in greeting. "It seems we cannot kill Blenar or bad Senar or women of the city today, Nugun. They are going to kill us."

Nugun shrugged. His massive body was thinner and reeked of filth and neglect. But he held himself as erect as ever, and his eyes were not dimmed. "Nugun know. But Nugun not die easy. Nugun fight."

"I will fight too," said Blade. "Perhaps we *can* kill some women." He was not optimistic, though. If he and Nugun tried to rush the archers across a hundred yards of open sand, they would indeed be sprouting arrows all over before they had gone very far. Their only hope was Truja's making her move, and he had no idea when that would be—or whether she would even be able to make it at all. To snatch Blade and Nugun from the middle of fifty archers would be a neat trick.

Idrana herself was striding out now to take her position in the circle of archers. Blade used the extra time to look carefully around him. The arena was no more than one-third full, yet that one-third must have held better than twenty thousand people. Blade noticed that most of the women wore sober browns, grays, and blacks, except for those who were showing off their loyalty to their faction. One whole section was filled with a solid mass of women in bright blue. Fifty yards farther on, he saw an equally large mass of equally bright green. Blade saw banners floating above the rear ranks of each faction and the glint of weapons on either side.

Idrana was in position now. Her voice rose high and clear, carrying across the arena and rising above the continued murmur of the crowd. "Oh, Sisters of the City of Brega, look upon us. This day, to Kina, Mother of All, we offer as sacrifice—these men." The trumpet sounded a third time, and the drums rolled, to be promptly drowned out by cheers and shouts.

Idrana stepped forward a pace, pulling an arrow from her quiver and nocking it to her bow. This was a signal for all the other archers around the arena to do the same.

Blade stared at the archers drawing a bead on him. Then he took a deep breath, grinned at Nugun, and made himself ready for what would literally be a dance of death.

16

Blade realized that the length of time he could dance before death came depended largely on the skill of Idrana and her archers. If they were good, he would not be hit as long as they were not aiming to hit him. But if they were inept, they would almost certainly not be able to avoid accidents. And the longer he stayed alive and on his feet, the longer Truja and her party would have to act.

Far away across the arena, he saw Idrana's arm draw back, then straighten. A faint black blur high against the blue sky told him of an arrow on its way. For a split second more, he stood still. Would Idrana be aiming directly at him, assuming he would dodge? Or would it appeal to her game-playing instincts to try to guess where he would jump and put her arrow there?

With a sudden snap of leg muscles, Blade swung to the left, going down and rolling. As he did so, the *Wheeeesh* of a descending arrow sounded loud in his ears. A split second later came a solid *whunk* as it plunged into the sand just behind where Blade had been standing. If he had not moved, it would have plunged down into his chest. That settled two things about Idrana. She could shoot well, and she would aim to hit—at least for now. Blade brushed the sand off his arms and looked at the distant circle again. Now the woman to the right of Idrana was drawing and shooting. Blade jumped back, not rolling this time. In the same moment he shouted "Move!" to Nugun. The Senar responded with a tremendous leap that

149

must have carried him a good eight feet. He nearly lost his balance on landing—but the arrow aimed at him whistled down and struck harmlessly ten feet away.

One by one, each woman around the circle took her shot. Before half the women had shot, it was obvious that they were alternating between Blade and Nugun. But still both of them went on moving each time they saw an arrow headed their way. Blade wasn't going to take chances on Idrana's playing tricks.

It was also obvious that Idrana had hand-picked her archers. Blade suspected that this was for reasons other than putting on a good show in the games. But they were certainly doing that. Each woman in the circle could obviously pick off a man-sized target at far more than a hundred yards' range. And equally obviously, they could also miss such a target with the same ease—as long as they wanted to. How long would they want to? And how long could Blade and Nugun keep up the leaps and bounds and rolls that had so far kept the arrows out of their flesh?

The second round was more than two-thirds done before any of the archers got an arrow anywhere close to the two men. Nugun was a fraction of a second slow in stepping off, and an arrow sliced down through his shoulder. It kept right on going into the ground, but left a bloody furrow in the hairy flesh. Nugun did not blink or wince at the pain. But he was a little quicker off the mark after that.

The second round was finished. A hundred arrows were now sticking in the sand in the center of the arena. The third round began. Soon the arrows sprouted still thicker.

The clusters of arrows were beginning to be a menace in themselves, as Blade realized when his foot caught in a bunch of three arrows when he leaped backward. He went sprawling. Only by a frantic twist and roll was he able to keep the next arrow from skewering his left leg. He rose, aware that he could no longer spring to his feet as fast. Sweat was pouring

150

off him, stinging his eyes and beginning to interfere with his vision. He wiped his forehead as best he could with the back of his hand.

As he did so, he heard a roar of pain and rage from Nugun. Blade opened his eyes, to see the Senar reach down and jerk an arrow out of his right calf. He raised the bloody thing high, then snapped it between thumb and forefinger and threw the pieces to the sand.

"Are you badly hurt?" Blade called.

The Senar growled and shook his head. "Not bad hurt for Senar. Blenar or woman curl up and die. "Not Nugun."

"Good." He waved encouragement to the Senar. The dance of death went on.

But it was not long before Blade realized that the arrow had done more damage than Nugun was willing to admit. A muscle torn, a major blood vessel open? More likely the former, since the bleeding didn't seem to be continuing. But Nugun was definitely favoring his right leg. Blade grimaced, realizing what this could mean, but he knew there was nothing he could do about it.

The third round came to an end and the fourth began without more damage to either Blade or Nugun. But there was no doubt that Nugun was beginning to slow. Apart from his wound, the Senar would have been treated even worse in the prison than Blade had been. And Blade knew what the treatment in prison had done to *his* strength and endurance. If he had not done his best to stay in shape, he knew he would have been shot down long ago.

As the fourth round continued, it seemed to Blade that the arrows were coming in faster, just as he and Nugun were beginning to slow down. Perhaps Idrana had decided to push the games toward a conclusion. And there would be no merciful shot aimed straight to the heart. Blade and Nugun would die bit by bit, pierced by arrow after arrow, and eventually killed only when they could no longer move and provide a

151

good show for the staring thousands in the stands of the arena. That fitted Idrana's nature.

Halfway through the fourth round, Blade took his first wound. An arrow raked along his ribs, leaving a bleeding red gouge. An inch deeper and it would have gone through muscles and blood vessels, slowing him disastrously. As it was, he could clench his teeth against the raw pain and continue to leap about as fast as his muscles and breath would let him.

Nugun was slowing even more. That he had not been badly hit yet was perhaps just good luck. Or perhaps the women knew that he was no longer such a challenging target. Although he was now almost lumbering about instead of leaping, Nugun still bore only two wounds.

The fourth round, the fifth. They had now been out here in the center of the arena, providing targets for Idrana's archers, for more than two hours. To Blade it seemed more like two days.

And then the sixth round started, and its fourth arrow plunged down out of the sky into Nugun's thigh. The Senar did not scream or shout or growl. His breath only hissed out between his teeth. He turned to Blade, and raised a hand in salute. Blade jumped aside from his own next arrow without taking his eyes off the Senar. A cold feeling was working inside him as he watched Nugun.

Then without a sound or a word, Nugun spun around and plunged toward the edge of the arena. He covered a quarter of the distance to the archers before they realized what he was doing. He covered another quarter before they could readjust their aim to a target running straight and fast across the sand. Nugun was halfway before the first arrow struck him. And even then it only tore through one arm. Nugun bellowed in rage, but did not stop, did not slow, did not even break his stride. If anything, he increased his pace. Blood from his wounded thigh pumped out, brightly visible to Blade in the center of the arena, but that also did not slow Nugun down.

152

Two more arrows struck him, one in the shoulder, one low in the back. Then he was too close to one side of the arena for the archers on the other side to fire at him without hitting their comrades. And the ones facing his charge were too unnerved to aim very well. Blade saw arrows flying wide by the dozens and had to step lively to avoid being hit by some that sailed out into the arena.

Only one more arrow struck Nugun, and that did not slow him down any more than the others had. Then he was at the edge of the arena, and the women were scattering to either side of him. They might have drawn their swords, but even from a hundred yards off Blade could see that they were too frightened.

They did not scatter fast enough. Nugun's arm swung out and down like a club, and a woman rolled in the dust and lay motionless. Another he smashed back against the wall with one blow, caving in her face with a second. Then he was up with Idrana, and Blade held his breath as Idrana's sword flashed. It leaped forward, driving low into Nugun's stomach. The Senar howled in agony, reeled, seemed about to double up. Idrana stepped back and motioned one of the other women to give the finishing blow.

The moment the woman was within reach, Nugun straightened up. His hands clutched the woman, lifting her off her feet, high over his head, then twisting her savagely. Like a broken doll she dropped to the sand, and Nugun dropped beside her, still writhing feebly. Another sword-thrust from Idrana ended his writhing.

Blade knelt on the sand, not risking the smallest move that the women might interpret as an attack. Nugun was gone, taking enemies with him as he had promised, and now Blade was alone. Alone to plan his escape as best he could—if the frightened and nervous women all around him did not simply let fly and drop him to the sand bristling with arrows.

How long he knelt there on the sand Blade never knew. But no arrows drove into his flesh or even whistled down near him. There was a vast silence throughout the whole arena. And then the silence was broken by an explosion of cheering.

Blade looked up. The entire Green section was on its feet, cheering and waving. They were not only waving their arms and their banners; they were waving handkerchiefs, scarves, or anything else white they could find. After a few moments, the cheering began to spread, and soon the whole arena was a mass of dancing white.

Blade kept his emotions under tight control. He recalled that in the Roman arena waving white was a request for mercy for the gladiators. He hoped it was the same here. But even if it were, he knew that there was more involved. The cheering and waving of the Greens had been too pat, too well timed. They had a place somewhere in Idrana's plans.

He realized that the archers were breaking out of their positions around the arena and coming toward him. Idrana was moving faster than the others, almost running across the sand, and reached him before the others did.

"Follow me, Blade," she hissed. "Keep your eyes open and your mouth shut. That Senar is dead and you can no longer do anything for him. But you can still be the man beside me as I rise to power in the city. Is that not better than lying dead on the sand?"

"It is."

"Good," she said, and then the other women were coming up. They swept Blade along as they ran toward the section of the arena stands where the two factions were. By the time the forty-odd survivors of Idrana's archers were gathered there, all the cheering had died.

Idrana stepped forward, lifting her bow in salute. In the front row of the Blue section, someone rose to her feet and bowed in return. In one swift, flowing motion, Idrana snatched an arrow from her quiver, nocked it, drew, and sent the arrow hurtling into the bowing woman. She doubled up and fell out of the stands onto the sand with a scream and a thud. Before

154

he had struck the ground, all the rest of Idrana's
archers had followed their leader's cue.

A hail of arrows whistled down into the Blue section.

17

Immediate and total pandemonium.

The shrieks and screams that rose from the Blue section were echoed seconds later from all around the arena. The women in the Green section rose in a body. Some of them scurried for the exits, while others drew their swords and started scrambling toward the Blues. Elsewhere in the stands women sat as if turned to stone; still others were dropping down onto the sand. Were they coming in to attack Idrana's archers or join them?

Blade didn't know, and badly wanted to. He wanted even more badly to find some place well out of the battle that would certainly be raging within a few minutes. If it was a place that offered an escape route, even better. He began looking around the arena.

Meanwhile, Idrana's archers kept up their fire, pumping flight after flight of arrows into the Blue section. That section was becoming a mass of writhing bodies and blood now, although a few of the Blue warriors had unlimbered their own bows and were shooting back.

As Blade ducked an arrow screaming toward him, he saw six women in the dirty gray clothes of manual workers leap down from the stands. The one in the lead waved her arms frantically at Blade. Blade stiffened as he recognized Truja.

He didn't wait. Shoving two of the archers aside, he dashed toward the approaching women. Truja leaped into the air in delight, then waved her arm at one of the open doors under the stands.

Blade and the women sprinted toward the door. As they ran, Blade heard a shriek of rage behind him— Idrana had seen her chosen male getting away. Blade tried to keep his head as low as possible.

But Idrana could not afford to waste arrows needed for the Blues on a fleeing male. Only a single flight came whistling over. All were aimed at Blade; none of them hit him, but by ill chance two struck one of Truja's women in the back. She screamed and staggered, then went down. Blade bent to help her up, but Truja stepped in front of him.

"No!" she snapped. Her hand darted in under her robes and drew out a sword. The woman writhing on the ground looked up and nodded. The sword plunged into the woman's neck, and she heaved convulsively in a death spasm and lay still. It was a quicker death than Idrana would have given her, and now she could not be tortured into betraying them.

The five surviving women and Blade charged into the door at a dead run, drawing their swords as they did so. The underground chamber was full of cages of Senar and chained women. The guards were already on the alert from the uproar above. They raised their swords as Truja's party charged in.

"Out of my way!" she snapped. "Business of the House!" "Business of the House" meant the affairs of the House of Fertility. None in the city except the Guardians of Fertility and Mistress herself might question these words. The guards drew back, the massive door rumbled open, and Truja led the way out into the underground corridor.

"Business of the House!" got them past the other two guard posts under the arena and several parties of armed women who were rushing about in a frenzy like ants in a broken nest. None of them paid any attention to Blade, although it was impossible to conceal him.

Truja grinned at that. "With everything else they've got on their minds now, I don't think they'd notice if you were fourteen feet tall and had two heads and long purple fur."

Then they were outside the Arena. The roar from inside was, if anything, growing louder. The women in the streets were staring toward it in curiosity and mounting fear. They were much too busy to notice the five women and the strange-looking Senar who slipped out of one of the underground passages.

Now the women stripped off their workers' robes. Under them they wore hunting costumes, complete with short, heavy bows and quivers. They tossed the robes to Blade, who made a rough cloak and loincloth out of them. Then all six headed for the gates of the city.

They covered the three miles at a dead run, without stopping once or slowing more often than the wretched streets underfoot required. After three weeks of confinement and nearly three hours in the arena, Blade found the run an ordeal. His heart seemed about to burst out through his ribs, and his lungs felt as if they were full of flaming-hot gas. Hot needles drove into the muscles of his legs. But from somewhere he found the strength to keep going.

The city gates were still open when Blade and the women came in sight of them. They promptly slowed down to a walk and tried to get their breathing back to normal.

The officer commanding the gate peered down out of the gatehouse at them as they approached. The uproar from the arena was beginning to be audible even here. And someone must have started setting fires. Several columns of black smoke were swirling up from the quarter of the city around the arena.

"What in the name of the Mother is happening?" the officer shouted.

"There's a riot at the arena," Truja called back.

"The Greens and the Blues?" the officer asked.

Truja shrugged. "Who else?"

"Damn them!" said the officer. "Where are you going?"

158

"Out to warn the farms and the patrols," Truja said. "The thing with us is a Senar the House of Fertility is sending out to a farm near Ufol Valley. He's an odd one, and they want to see how well he can work."

"All right," the officer said, and waved them on through.

Once out of sight of the gate, the six broke into a run again. This time they kept running until they did not have the breath left to run any farther, then slowed down to a fast walk. They did not stop until they had covered five or six miles and the city was only a patch of darkness on the horizon behind them. They took shelter in one of the ruined buildings of the old city and collapsed.

Eventually Blade found the breath to ask a few questions and Truja found the breath to answer them.

"How are things at the camp?"

"I wouldn't know. I left for the city only two days after you were captured. As much as we wanted to get you back, getting the sisters out of the city was more important."

Blade shrugged. "I can't blame you. Nugun and I shouldn't have let ourselves get captured the way we did. Did you get the women out?"

"All but a handful, yes. Most of them will probably be at the camp by the time we get there."

"How many fighters?"

"Four hundred or more."

"Good. That may be the largest body of city fighting women left by the time the Blues and the Greens get through slaughtering each other."

"I know. And Rilgon's army is less than a week from the walls."

"Has *any* word of it come to the city?"

"Not that I heard. And would the Greens have struck if they had heard of Rilgon's approach?"

"I don't know," said Blade. "Their war leader Idrana is an ambitious fanatic. I'm not sure it would have made any difference."

"May Mother Kina curse her," said Truja slowly pounding her clenched fist on the ground.

An hour later they were all sufficiently rested to be able to move out again. They did not run or trot now, but Truja still set a brisk pace along the road.

They were about two hours farther on when they saw a cloud of dust on the road ahead. They stopped, and Truja told Blade to slip into the bushes that bordered the road. He obeyed, and from his hiding place he heard and saw what followed.

There were four women, each wearing a large yellow triangle on their tunics. They approached at a run, and as they did Blade could see that they had been running for a long time. Their faces were gray with fatigue and caked with dust, their eyes stared blindly, and their tongues protruded through cracked lips.

They slowed slightly as they saw Truja.

"Hail, Messengers! What news?"

One of the four took a deep breath. "There is an army of Senar in the land! Thousands of them, thousands! They are coming to the city. Mother Kina save us, for we are all lost!"

"Nonsense!" said Truja sharply. "Mother Kina watches over those who keep her Law—and sharpen their swords in good time. Go on to the city, and tell them that also!"

The women nodded and got into their stride again. They went pounding away down the road and soon were again a cloud of dust on the horizon. Blade stepped out into the road. Truja was standing there numbly, her face working and tears glistening in the corner of her eyes.

"Why couldn't they have come just a *few hours* earlier?" she groaned. "Brega is doomed, doomed!"

"As you yourself said—nonsense!" retorted Blade. "Right now the best thing we can do is get back to the camp as fast as possible. We can't do anything by ourselves."

It took them barely two days to get back to the

160

camp of the Purple River fighters by the War House. Truja kept Blade and the women moving on hour after hour, as if every extra step they took crushed one of Rilgon's Senar underfoot. Like the run through the city, the march was an ordeal for Blade. But again, he kept on going.

When they reached the camp on the morning of the third day, there were surprises on both sides. Himgar and the others had long since given up both Truja and Blade for dead, and were delighted to see them tramping out of the forest. On the other hand, they were far from delighted with the news that the women of the city had decided to fight a civil war just at the moment that Rilgon had decided to strike. Himgar, even more high-strung and nervous than usual, nearly burst into tears at that news.

For Blade and Truja, the surprise was to find that nearly five hundred farm women had joined the Purple River camp. And more were coming in every day. Some of them had been driven from their farms by Rilgon's army and lost everything but the desire for revenge. Others were simply the independent-minded. The women of the farms had never much trusted the city, always kept the Laws of Mother Kina according to their own lights, and tended to rely more on strong arms than on strong customs. As far as they could see, the Purple River people now had the strongest arms around.

"Yes, you are the best fighters now," one of them said to Blade. "And more will think that when they hear how the Blues and Greens fight in the city. The others will come here, and if they do not come here, they will tell what they see and hear."

In other words, thought Blade, they would be willing to act as scouts for us. They would give the Purple River army an enormous advantage. Blade doubted if Rilgon and his Blenar knew any more about scouting than they did about nuclear physics. And the women of the city—well, they seemed to be good enough fighters individually. But had they ever fought a regular battle or campaign? Of course there was the factional civil war that Idrana had just started No doubt it would give many of the fighting women of the city experience in large-scale combat. But would it leave any reasonable number of them alive, to profit by that experience and use it against Rilgon? Blade wondered.

He went directly to Himgar and broached the notion of using the farm women as scouts. The War Councilor was dubious.

"That could mean word of our presence getting to the city," he said. "If our scouts betray us—"

"You seem to trust the women in camp," Blade interrupted.

"Yes, but they are under our eyes all the time. These—they would be beyond our control."

"So what?" said Blade, annoyed. "The women of the city certainly aren't going to be able to attack us before Rilgon's army arrives. And we're going to have to deal with the women as equals sooner or later, whether we trust them or not."

Himgar's eyebrows went up. "Has Truja converted you to her views? Do you think we should help the women of the city defeat Rilgon and then negotiate with them?"

Blade had to be silent for only a few seconds before he found his answer. "Yes. The farm women have come to us in the belief that we would do this. And so have most of the women from the city. I think both would leave us at once if we simply broke camp and headed north. They would try to fight Rilgon by themselves, they would lose, and they would die. And then so would the city and everything that we might make of it. But if we stay and fight—"

"How can we?" said Himgar, half-despairing.

Blade did not attempt to conceal the scorn in his voice. "You call yourself a War Councilor, and you ask that question? Truja has pointed the way. We attack them from the rear. With the farm women scouting for us, we will have no problems finding that rear."

"But—"

"Himgar, if you do not agree to fight Rilgon, I will join Truja. We will lead the farm women and the city women away, and you and the rest of the Purple River people can all go to the devil!" He caught his breath. "You know that I have even less reason to love the women of the city than you do. But I can see that they are worth saving, in spite of that. You cannot, and you are not wise."

Himgar was silent for a much longer time than Blade had been. Finally he said quietly, "I have heard of how Truja gave you leadership of the scouts. Would you like to become War Councilor of our people in my place? If we are going to do what you suggest, perhaps you should lead."

"No, Himgar, I am only a warrior from a distant land, and most of your people do not know me well enough to trust me. But I will stand at your right hand and give you all the advice you need."

"In other words, you will run the battle?"

"Yes," said Blade.

Himgar shrugged. "So be it. I trust you enough so that I trust your plan, for all that you can do to carry it out. But there are others who may have something to say."

"I know. Rilgon. And the women of the city."

Blade wasted no time in setting up his network of scouts. Even though Melyna was among the Purple River army's fighting women, he had little time or attention to spare for her. And there would have been little privacy for them even if he had found the time. The Purple River army and all its assorted allies overflowed the War House and spread out into the forest around it.

It helped matters that Rilgon's army sat down for nearly a week at a point three days' march west of the camp. The Senar and even the Blenar indulged in an orgy of gluttony, rape, pillage, and destruction.

163

"Rilgon either has no control over his army or doesn't care," said Blade when he heard that news. "Half of them won't want to move on again. Those that do will have only half their minds on fighting." And in fact Rilgon's army was distinctly smaller when it moved on at the end of the week.

It was moving along a course that would take it well south of the camp. That was good news for Blade. There were now just over three thousand men and women in the camp. He did not want to try moving such a large and mixed group across country with an enemy—in fact two enemies—nearby.

Rilgon's army lumbered past to the south and settled down again, a day's march farther on toward the city. In the camp, tension mounted by the hour. The sound of weapons being sharpened rose loud enough to be heard miles away. But all the farm women in the area had either fled or joined the camp. There was no one to hear. Only the scouts moved back and forth across the countryside, bringing and sending word.

It was on the fourth day that they brought the long-awaited word. The army of the city—Blues and Greens together—was marching out. Tomorrow it would be up to Rilgon's army. And the day after that it would fight.

So Blade and Himgar and Truja gave their orders also. And their army too marched out, gathering up the scouts as it went. It moved forward—into the rear of the enemy.

18

Once more Blade was perched on a branch of a tall tree. But this time he was not ten feet up, but nearly a hundred. If he fell off now, he would *not* have a soft landing. But it was an excellent place from which to observe Rilgon's army assembling for battle.

It was an act of pure charity to call what Rilgon was assembling out there on the plain to the east an army. The only part of it that had ever heard of military formation was the two-thousand odd Blenar in the center. The rest of the "army" consisted of Senar, arranged in a series of lumpy masses rather like beads on a string, with a thousand or so in each "bead."

The complete force stretched nearly two miles from north to south and numbered somewhere around fifteen thousand of both races. That was a full one-third less than Rilgon had originally led out. Of the missing third (mostly Senar), some had died at the hands of farmers. Some had lost heart and started back for home. And some had grown too fond of sloth and debauchery to want to keep up with the army.

But fifteen thousand men, armed and even slightly trained, was still a good-sized force. To meet it Blade and Himgar had no more than three thousand. On the other side of Rilgon's line, Idrana was leading up a slightly smaller force from the citiy. Perhaps she was filled with distrust for most of the fighting women of the city, or perhaps with contempt for the enemy.

Neither the women of the city nor their enemies knew about the Purple River army as yet. Rilgon had chosen to draw up his army with a thick stand of woods a mile to their rear. No doubt he thought it would help stiffen the Senar to know that in a pinch retreat into the forest that was their home was always possible. Perhaps he was right.

But certainly the forest that was intended to stiffen the Senar was also perfect for hiding the Purple River army. Within a hundred yards of the base of the tree where Blade was perched lay almost three thousand men and women. None moved, none spoke; the preparation of weapons had been completed last night. They were waiting for two things—Idrana's army to engage Rilgon's, and Blade's signal for *them* to charge out of the forest and take Rilgon in the rear.

Right now Blade was keeping his eye on a flag that bobbed on a high pole beyond Rilgon's line. It was a bright green flag with a stylized woman's head on it—the Mother's Banner of the Greens. Blade shook his head. Idrana was so committed to her faction that she would go into battle for the life of her city under it. If she had any Blues at all with her, it was only because they set the survival of their city above vengeance for their slaughtered leaders.

Now the banner was waving up and down, as though the bearers were moving over rough ground. Then it stopped. Blade saw a shiver run down Rilgon's line, and beyond it a ripple of movement. Idrana's army was getting ready for its first movement.

Suddenly a flight of arrows was in the air, looking like a wisp of black smoke from this far away. But before they came down, Rilgon's men had reacted. They snatched up their shields and held them up in front of them. Most of the arrows sank harmlessly into the tough leather. Blade saw a few swirls among the Senar as the careless or the over-confident went down. But very few.

Score one to Rilgon. Against those shields, the women of the city could pour in flight after flight of arrows without much weakening their enemy. Rilgon had hit on the best way of forcing Idrana's women to

166

close the distance. Now—how long would it take Idrana to realize that?

The duel of arrow against shield went on for a good ten minutes. The city banner did not move at all during that time. Then the air between the two armies was suddenly clear. A moment later the banner started forward again.

It was moving straight for the mass of Blenar in the middle of Rilgon's line. Blade cursed out loud and pounded his fist against the branch as he realized what Idrana was doing—and what folly it was. Idrana was charging the enemy's center. No doubt she thought that smashing the enemy's best troops would smash the whole army. But those same best troops could put up the best fight. And while they held Idrana's army in one place, the two wings of Senar, many thousands strong, could swing in and surround the women.

It was already happening, in fact. There was a continuous glitter of dancing steel in the center of the field, where Blenar were going into action. And there was unmistakable movement all along the lines of Senar. The dark masses were in motion, swinging in toward the center, spear-points glittering above them. Blade saw arrows fly again, but it was too late for that now. Within minutes the masses of Senar would be on the women, jamming them together so the archers would have no room to shoot.

It was time and more than time for the Purple River army to go into action. As he scrambled down the tree, Blade could not help wondering if he had waited too long. He dropped the last ten feet in a single bound, rolled, sprang to his feet, and shouted:

"All right—follow me! Center, hit the Blenar. Wings, get the Senar!"

He heard his shout and his orders relayed away through the trees. Then he heard the clatter of weapons and the thud of feet as three thousand men and women rose and began to move.

Blade crashed through bushes and leaped gullies. He was already moving at a dead run when he burst out of the trees, both swords drawn. He tore across the mile of open ground between the trees and the enemy at a pace that would have done credit to a track runner. Behind him came three hundred of the best fighters of the Purple River and the city women, none of them moving much slower than Blade himself. Himgar was in the lead.

They did not waste breath shouting as they raced across the fields without slowing or stopping. The farther they got before the enemy noticed what was coming up in his rear, the better. Half a mile gone, half a mile to go. Blade sailed over a hedge four feet high as if it had been a mere ripple in the ground, nearly tumbled headlong, kept on going.

A quarter of a mile to go now, only a couple more minutes. Behind him Blade could see that almost the whole Purple River army was out of the trees. On either side farm women and the rest of the Purple River fighters were already spreading out, to curl round the masses of Senar.

And now, finally, the rear ranks of the Blenar were turning— around, pointing, and beginning to shout the alarm. No need for silence any more. Blade opened his mouth and let out a maniacal screech; it was echoed by all the men and women running behind him. It seemed to rise up to the sky and bounce back, down onto the enemy ranks. Blade saw some of them wince.

Only a hundred yards to go. Blade waved both swords over his head and screamed again. He increased his speed still more, covered the last few yards at a sprinter's pace, and crashed into the enemy's ranks like a battering ram.

Seconds later the men and women behind Blade did the same. They came in so fast that they simply bowled over a good many of their opponents, smashing them to the ground and trampling them underfoot. Most of the Blenar had formed a shield wall facing the women of the city and were holding well against them. But a shield wall faces only one way. And Blade had launched his attack from another direction.

168

Through the Blenar ranks Blade slashed, both swords leaping and flashing with terrifying speed and thrusting and slashing with terrifying effect. He killed or crippled five men before he was even aware of it, his flawless training and lightning reflexes taking control of his brain. Then he became fully conscious of where he was and what he was doing. He began to carve his way forward, not as fast as before, but even more surely.

The Blenar were trying to turn and face the attack in their rear. But they could not weaken the wall against Idrana's women too much. Within minutes Blade's attack was packing the Blenar so tightly that only the front rank could move or use their weapons. And a single rank of Blenar could not hope to stand against the fury and skill of Blade and his comrades.

Blade saw Himgar hack through the shaft of a spear with one stroke, and the neck of the spearsman with the return slash. A Blenar with two swords ran at him while he was killing the first one. But Truja was fighting on Himgar's flank, and she stepped across to cover the Councilor, thrusting the attacker in the stomach as she did so. The second Blenar sank down on the trampled and blood-smeared grass almost beside the first.

Then a solid mass of Blenar was coming at Blade, and he and the people on either side of him had to give way for a moment. But only for a moment. As the Blenar pushed forward, the attackers curled around them and drove in behind them. Again Blade was the first to make the move and he did so with even more determination than usual. In the center of the Blenar he could see the bulky shape of Rilgon himself.

Blade hacked his way past three successive Blenar, not even trying to kill them. He was satisfied with getting them out of his way and leaving them for his comrades to kill. His goal was Rilgon—the heart and brains of the enemy.

But as Blade drove into the ranks of the enemy, he found his own arms had less room to swing and strike. As he came within striking distance of Rilgon, a dying Blenar reeled into him, pinning his left arm against his side for a moment. At the same moment Rilgon lashed out and down with his long, jeweled sword. Blade's long-sword snapped up just in time to keep the blow from splitting his skull, but the point ripped open the scalp on the right side of his head. Blade felt the pain sear and the blood start flowing. With a convulsive jerk of his left arm, he shoved the dying Blenar away. Then his short sword lunged forward, driving in under Rilgon's shield. Blade felt it sink into flesh, saw Rilgon grit his teeth and let his breath out in a hiss.

Rilgon's long-sword whistled high, coming over and down, and again Blade blocked it. The clang of steel on steel half-deafened him. He swung his own long-sword around and brought it in from the side, hoping to draw Rilgon's shield out of position.

He did. If Rilgon had ever fought before against a thrusting sword, he gave no sign of it now. His shield swung unnecessarily wide to meet Blade's slash. Blade's long-sword crashed into the edge of the shield. At the same moment Blade's short-sword plunged into Rilgon's unguarded side, vanishing halfway up to the hilt.

Rilgon gasped, coughed, and reeled. His shield sagged and dropped away. He lurched back, the short-sword still deep in his side, and coughed again, spraying blood all over Blade. Before Rilgon could do anything else, Blade's sword came down for the last time, with a force that would have sent it through a steel post. It went through Rilgon's neck as though the neck had been a twig. The severed head flew into the air and dropped at Blade's feet. As the body with its spouting neck toppled, Blade jabbed his long-sword into the head and raised it high.

He took a deep breath, and roared, "Rilgon's men—see your leader—he is *dead!* Now it is your turn—all of you!" Cheers went up from the Purple River army on either side of Blade and behind him. Then Blade was too busy coping with a fresh rush of still-fighting Blenar to shout again or to see the effects of his first cry.

In fact, for a long time he was too busy to see or hear anything that was not immediately in front of him. At least it seemed like a long time—entire hours of slashing and thrusting and parrying with his sword or blocking with a shield he snatched up from a fallen Blenar.

It could not have been hours, however. In fact, it was probably only a few minutes. Certainly the whole battle from first arrow to last flurry of sword-cuts lasted less than an hour. While Blade's attack was confusing and confounding Rilgon's center and disposing of Rilgon, the rest of his army was smashing into the Senar on either flank. The Senar's new fighting skills were no match for the Purple River warriors in their armor, the trained fighting women of the city, or the farm women fighting for vengeance.

The Senar were already crumbling when the word ran through their ranks that Rilgon was dead. Then they not only crumbled; they collapsed. They began to break away and try to run. As they did so, everybody with a bow unlimbered it and began picking them off one by one. Those without bows joined in the attack on the rapidly diminishing force of Blenar in the center. Gradually the Blenar shrank away to nothing.

It was then that Blade made his way forward, over the piled bodies, toward where the women of the city stood in a tight circle around their standard. He could see that there were a good many less than three thousand of them now. Hundreds of the women lay dead amid the bodies of their enemies. Many of those still on their feet were blood-stained and pale. But there was one more woman of the city who would have to die before there could be peace in Brega.

Idrana.

He was within a hundred yards of the women's lines when he saw a familiar long-limbed figure sprawled on the ground off to his left. He turned and quickened his step, came up to her, knelt down beside her. There was nothing more to do for Idrana—or to her. A Senar spear had transfixed her from back to front as neatly as a pin impaling a butterfly. Blade felt empty of any emotion as he stared down at the still, pale face.

Then he heard a voice calling softly, from beyond Idrana.

"Blade—here."

He raised his head—and started. Twenty feet away, Truja lay on her stomach, raising a pale, pain-twisted face toward Blade. In two bounds he was beside her, kneeling again. She tried to keep her head up, could not find the strength, and instead rolled over on her side. The movement brought a gasp of agony and revealed a gaping wound that ran from breast to groin. It was obvious that Truja had only a few minutes to live.

She was plucking at his trousers, trying to get his attention again.

"Yes, Truja."

"Tell—Himgar. No time—wish I had—"

"I know. I'll tell him. You rest."

"No. Idrana—"

"She's dead."

"I know. Put—spear—myself. Looked like—Senar did it. Got—me—with sword—didn't step back. But she's—dead. Had to—honor—future of Brega City—oh, Mother Kina!" The last was almost a scream. Truja clenched her teeth and for a moment her body contorted like a worm on a hook. Then she slumped back, blood trickling from her mouth. A moment later her eyes drifted closed, and her breathing stopped.

19

Blade became aware of someone standing behind him. He turned around, and saw Himgar. The man's face was frozen in the expression of one who would like to cry but can't spare the time or energy. His voice was steady as he said:

"Blade, the battle is over. And our victory—your victory—is complete."

Blade straightened up, rubbed his smarting eyes, and looked around the battlefield. At least the first part of Himgar's statement was correct. There were no organized groups of the enemy anywhere in sight. Miles away in all directions Blade could see little scattered groups of fugitive Senar. All of them were running as fast as they could and making no attempt to turn and fight their pursuers. Closer in, where the main battle had been fought, there was not a single square yard of ground without at least one body. Most of the bodies —men, women, Blenar, Senar—were motionless and already stiffening. Some were still writhing and twisting. Blade saw both Purple River and city fighters searching out the living, ending their struggles if they were enemy, trying to help them if they were friendly. The fighters of the two allies were also watching each other cautiously. Their shared victory was not enough to create mutual trust after so many centuries of mutual hostility and misunderstanding.

But that trust would have to come sooner or later, or all the dead of the city and the Purple River today would have died for no purpose. Blade sighed. The second part of Himgar's remarks was hardly correct.

173

"The victory is not complete," he said sharply. "We still have to win over the city, the way Truja hoped we would be able to do. And that will take more work."

Himgar almost groaned out loud. Blade couldn't really blame him. He himself was fighting an almost overwhelming temptation to sit down and rest. It took an effort even to think about doing anything else.

But Blade found the energy to think, and to plan, and eventually to act. His orders went out, and bit by bit they were obeyed. The bodies were piled up and parties sent to cut wood for funeral pyres. The wounded of both allied armies were placed under the care of the doctors from the city, with their more advanced knowledge.

Meanwhile the fleeing Senar and their pursuers both passed out of sight. Between those pursuers and the local farm women, few of the Senar would escape. With his memories of Nugun, Blade could not help wishing there was something else to do with the Senar than mercilessly slaughter them. Some day the new society growing in Brega should be able to reach out and take in even the Senar. Perhaps its medicine could discover and eradicate whatever malignant influence distorted their bodies and stunted their minds.

But that was for a future many generations distant. For the moment, the fewer Senar who got back to their homes, the longer it would be before they considered another attack on the city. And the city would need a good many years of peace.

There were still a fair number of women in the city who seemed determined to continue living in the past, of course. The battle had not been over for two hours before some of the Blues and Greens were using up the last of their energy slashing at each other. Blade shouted angry orders, and the farm women waded in with their tools and clubs like riot police, beating and shoving the combatants apart.

Blade noticed, in fact, that the farm women were

almost strutting in front of their sisters from the city. They, the despised and half-heretical women of the westlands, had seen what had to be done more clearly than the wise women of the city. And they had done more of what needed to be done than their sisters had, shedding their blood more freely in doing so. Or so it seemed to them, at least. Blade hoped the farm women would not strut enough to cause bad blood between them and the city.

But that was something which he could not possibly hope to control. What he could do, and had to do now, was to enter the city and approach the House of Fertility. Perhaps he could enter it, if the Mistress and the guardians were so disposed. He could certainly speak with them, tell them about the new society which had been hammered out in blood that morning.

Himgar was unable to speak for nearly a minute after Blade threw out the suggestion. And all he could say when he did find his voice was, "Why?"

Blade shrugged. "If the women are planning treachery—well, I know the city, and I have a good chance of running or fighting. Also, I can perhaps understand what the Mistress will say better than others of your people."

"Possibly. But—to enter the House of Fertility—?"

"It will have to be done sooner or later," said Blade wearily. "And the sooner the better. If we move in before the women of the city recover from their shock, we will be in a much stronger position. I'm willing to risk having to fight my way out of the city again, but I'll be damned if I want to have to fight my way *into* it."

Himgar had to concede that point. An hour later Blade had picked seventy volunteers for his expedition to the city, including Melyna. And an hour after that, the seventy-one were on the march.

Although they had all fought through the battle, Blade pushed his volunteers along as ruthlessly as he pushed himself. He had meant what he said to Himgar

175

about the need for haste, before the women of the city recovered from the shock. And there was another reason for haste, one that he could not very well admit to anyone. His time in this dimension could not last much longer. He badly wanted to take something home besides a tale of more than usually hair-raising adventures among more than usually strange peoples.

Some of them were almost asleep on their feet, but all seventy were still with Blade when he marched up to the main gate of the city. It was just before dawn of the next morning, with the sky only beginning to turn gray. Blade stepped forward and hailed the gate. He was not sure that the response would not be a flight of arrows. And he would not have particularly blamed the women if it had been.

But it was not. By good fortune the commander of the gate was the same officer who had been on duty the day of Blade's flight from the city. She even recognized him in the dim light. Her voice held a strange, almost bantering note as she spoke to him.

"Well—if it isn't the strange Senar. Have you come to gloat over what you have done to the city?"

"No, I have not. I have come to pay my respects to the Mistress of Fertility, and if possible to enter the House of Fertility."

This produced a prolonged and total silence from the gate tower. Eventually there were mutterings and murmurings, as though a debate were going on among the guards on duty. Then the commander's voice came again.

"Enter the city, man, and trust us at the gate for anything we can control. But I cannot aid your suit before the Mistress. Still less can we protect you from any women in the city who may take vengeance for"—the officer's voice choked—"seeing the Law of Mother Kina fall down about them." Her voice broke, faded away, and then there was the sound of sobbing in the darkness above.

Blade did not feel like waiting around to witness

the officer's humiliation. As soon as the gate opened, he led his followers through it at a trot and into the city.

It would not have mattered whether the women of the city were friendly or not, for the streets were almost totally deserted. At least there were few living women out and about, and these dove for cover when Blade's grim and well-armed seventy came marching past. But there were a good many bodies still littering the streets. A nauseating miasma of death and decay and stark fear hung over the city.

So did a terrible and sullen silence. Occasionally moans and cries floated out of half-open windows, and once or twice drunken laughter. Once the marching column had to scatter to avoid a shower of tiles hurled down from above amid mocking laughter. Blade's party did not even bother to send any arrows back. It seemed that the women of the city had crawled away into hiding like wounded animals, to try to come to terms with their grief and shock.

They came up to the House of Fertility at a brisk trot and formed a ring around the broad wooden stairs. Blade walked up those stairs with Melyna one step behind him and struck the high silver door three times with the hilt of his sword.

"Who craves entrance?" came a booming voice from above.

"Blade, a warrior of the Purple River, to speak with the Mistress."

As Blade had expected, this produced another of those long silences. This one stretched on for nearly ten minutes. The people in the street below began to fidget. The sky had grown noticeably lighter by the time the silence was broken.

It was broken by the huge silver door beginning to slide open, smoothly and with only the faintest of grating sounds. There was a concerted gasp from the people below. The door slid into a wall slot, leaving an arched opening thirty feet high and forty feet wide.

177

Against the pale gold light filling the opening Blade saw a small figure silhouetted.

It was a woman, the smallest that Blade had seen in Brega. She was several inches under five feet tall and looked at least a hundred years old. Her hair was silvery-white, making a striking contrast with her plain black robe.

"You are Blade." It was a statement, not a question.

"I am."

"I am the Mistress. Enter the House, and the woman with you also."

"My—"

"They may wait. No harm will come to them, the city being as it is."

Blade hesitated for a moment, but only for a moment. A trap? Not likely. The Mistress looked about as capable of setting a trap as of beating him in hand-to-hand combat. He stepped forward, Melyna followed him more slowly, and the door slid shut behind them.

There was no trap for Blade and Melyna in the House of Fertility. Instead, there were three hours of tramping endless corridors floored in shining black and walled in equally glossy white. Three hours of following the tireless footsteps of the diminutive Mistress from one gold-vaulted chamber to another. Three hours of marvels—enough to give Home Dimension doctors ten years' work in analyzing any one of them and the people of Brega a thousand years' work in relearning how to use them all.

Outside, Blade knew that daylight must long since have come. Perhaps the city had awakened from its daze, and his party was fighting for their lives against the enraged women. The Mistress assured him that this was not so. But how could she know? The walls of the house seemed thick enough to resist a bomb, let alone shut out the noise of any battle.

And then finally they came to the Chambers of Nurture. Row on row of tubular glass incubators filled it, stretching away into the shadows at the far end. In

178

almost every incubator was a baby—naked, healthy pink, sometimes kicking small limbs. At the end of each incubator sat a small gold box about a foot long, with a dozen or so flickering lights on the top.

The Mistress pointed. "As soon as an infant can live outside the womb, it is taken from its Brood Mother and brought here. It is placed in a Nurturing Cell, and the Watcher for the Cell is activated. For—"

"The Watcher is—what?" Blade stared at the gleaming cylinders and the gold boxes.

"The gold box. It senses any change in the condition of the baby, and—"

But Blade was not listening to the explanation of the Mistress. Pain—raw, tearing pain—was beginning to pound in his head, pound at his brain. Lord Leighton's computer was only seconds from taking him. His time in this dimension was coming to an end, and he still had nothing to show for it.

The Watcher! Perhaps it was worth—

"Mistress!" He fought to keep his voice under control. "Could I see one of the Watchers? I want to—look at one—more closely. In—my—land—" He did not want to just run over and snatch a Watcher, risking the precarious peace to satisfy his own curiosity, or even to carry out his mission!

The Mistress looked at Blade strangely, for his voice sounded distorted and pain-ridden even to his own ears. But she stepped over to one of the vacant Cells and picked up its Watcher. She came back to Blade, saying, "To activate it, one—"

But Blade could hold back no longer. His arms reached out; his hands clutched the box so hard that he felt the thin metal bend under his grip. The Mistress stared wide-eyed, while Melyna gaped in growing terror.

Blade clutched the Watcher to his chest just as the pain reached a peak. He knew his legs were buckling under him, but he managed to throw himself backward instead of falling on the Watcher. His head struck the floor with a crash and pain flamed through him. But he did not relax his grip on the Watcher. He was still holding his arms clamped around it when the pain washed over him and carried him away into blackness.

J stubbed out his cigar in the marble ashtray and pushed the manila folder across the teakwood desk at Blade.

"There's your copy, Richard. It's only a preliminary assessment, of course, but—"

"What is the Watcher, then?"

J began to rummage in one drawer of the desk for another cigar as he spoke. "Apparently it is an extremely complex protein compound, only one very small step below living matter. That is a rather impressive achievement, all by itself."

"There's more?"

"Yes. Remember what the Mistress said—about the Watcher sensing changes in the baby's condition? Well, that's what it does. In some way it undergoes subtle chemical changes whenever there is a deterioration in the vital signs of any human being it is—watching."

"A sort of robot nurse, in other words?"

"All that—and more besides. The people in Brega must have been very close to creating artificial life—completely synthetic artificial life—when the disaster came upon them. But at least we've got the Watcher."

"By good luck and a margin of about ten seconds, yes."

There was an edge in Blade's voice as he said that which made J look sharply at the younger man. Blade showed no sign of injury from his trip to Brega except a small bandage over his scalp wound. He was tanned even more than usual, and seemed to have been toughened and trimmed down. That was it—Blade was looking too lean, too stripped down to the basics. J swallowed. This would be a delicate question.

"Is—something particular bothering you—about the trip to Brega?"

Blade shrugged. "Not this trip all by itself. But this on top of all the others—I'm getting tired of relying so much on luck."

"You don't rely on it, Richard. You—"

"Please—spare me the lecture about making my own luck." Blade paused. "Sorry, sir. I shouldn't have snapped back that way. But—sometimes I just get the feeling that I'm going around in circles. A lot of work is going into—what? So far there hasn't been a single worthwhile development from everything I've brought back."

It was J's turn to shrug. "I know. I don't like it any better than you do. But the scientists aren't magicians. And if large-scale teleportation ever gets perfected—"

"And how long is that going to take?" said Blade. He took a long pull at his Scotch.

"Lord Leighton estimates—not more than another five years."

Blade was so obviously not making the obvious retort—"I may be dead by then"—that J felt slightly embarrassed. To cover that feeling, he lit a cigar from the drawer and took a few puffs on it.

"I'm not asking to be taken off the project," Blade went on. "It's too important for England—and that means I'm too important for England. I can't indulge myself—although I can't pretend any more that the idea isn't getting tempting." When Blade mentioned England, there was a world of meaning in the word, meaning which would have sounded like parody or satire if anybody else had said it. But Blade and J—and Lord Leighton and the Prime Minister—saw eye-to-eye on this, if on little else.

"But I *am* going to be losing efficiency if I have to carry the whole burden alone too much longer. More than another three or four trips, I suspect. I'm not particularly interested in going back to some places I've already been. So as far as I'm concerned, you can shove Controlled Return up the flue. But I very badly want and need an alternate—or at least a partner. Somebody to guard my back. Consider that suggestion I put in my report."

"About checking for possible *woman* partners?"

"Yes. You seem to have drawn a blank with the men so far. I admit women tend to be at a slight physical disadvantage. But suppose they turn out to have more tolerance for the *mental* stresses of a dimensional transfer?"

"A rather large supposition, one would think."

"Possibly. But certainly worth exploring."

"And just as certainly better than risking the whole project, or at least delaying it. I take your point. Very well, I'll extend the search net to qualified women. I doubt if there are more than two or three hundred in the whole free world worth examining. So it shouldn't take that long."

"I hope not. And—speaking of women—"

"How is Elizabeth?"

"Yes." Blade's face was slightly flushed. Thank God that Richard *could* show some concern for someone like Elizabeth! J had met—and even employed—ice-cold killing machines—too many of them. But he had never felt comfortable around them.

"We pushed our inquiry about Elizabeth as far as we could. And as far as we pushed it, her story stood up. So—she's on her way to Canada by now, and there's no reason to think that she won't be perfectly safe. She'll probably be married and have a child or two within five years."

"I hope so. She was—it was almost obscene, using somebody like that in the game. What turned up about the people behind her, by the way?"

"That we're still having to push along, I'm afraid. Other than the guns, there are no *definite* signs of any Soviet role in the whole affair."

"But plenty of vague hints around the edges?"

"I'm afraid so. The whole project is under a Grade Two Security Alert for the time being."

"Damn," said Blade.

J grinned. "Richard, *you* get to escape into Dimension X, where nobody has ever heard of the cold war or security alerts. *I* have to stay behind and hold a secure base for you while you travel."

Blade nodded slowly. "You—and me—and Lord Leighton—we're all linked together in this. Like a set of Siamese triplets."

J could not say anything against that.